OUR ROCK AND OUR SALVATION

HUGH MACDONALD

Our rock and our salvation
Text © 2021 by Hugh MacDonald
ISBN 9781-77366-091-2

Cover design and interior layout by Cassandra Aragonez
Editing by Penelope Jackson
Copyediting by Jennifer Graham

Printed in Canada by Marquis

Library and Archives Canada Cataloguing in Publication

＼

Title: Our rock and our salvation / Hugh MacDonald.
Names: MacDonald, Hugh, 1945- author.
Description: Book 3 in the Last wild boy trilogy.
Identifiers: Canadiana (print) 20210322993 |
Canadiana (ebook) 20210323035 | ISBN 9781773660912
(softcover) | ISBN 9781773660929 (HTML)

Classification: LCC PS8575.D6306 O97 2021 |
  DDC jC813/.54—dc23

The publisher acknowledges the support of the Government of
Canada, the Canada Council for the Arts and the Province of
Prince Edward Island for our publishing program.

P.O. Box 22024
Charlottetown, Prince Edward Island
C1A 9J2
Acornpress.ca

ACORNPRESS

To all readers, writers, publishers, and teachers
dedicated to the earth and all creatures living on it.

Chapter 1:
New Threats

On the day Adam celebrated his fifteenth birthday, his father, Mabon, and mother, Nora, called everyone in the newcomer community together and explained how they had spoken to representatives of the forest people's tribal council, who managed the complex relationships between the various families and groups that made up its surrounding population. Mabon and Nora had been asked to attend meetings to discuss common problems but had declined the kind offer. They had suggested the names of two younger people instead.

"That's crazy, Mabon," Adam said, his dark brown eyes intense and serious. "Me, a fifteen-year-old kid, on the council with the elders?"

"Why crazy?" Mabon said, showing his crooked smile. "They thought it was a great idea. I told them how smart you were and how well you could write and understand and explain yourself to them and report to us. It's an important job."

"What does Mom think?"

"We both think it's a great idea."

"Will one of you come with me to the meetings?"

"No," Mabon said. "They want your fresh ideas and energy."

"But I don't want to go there alone," said Adam. "I hardly know any of the forest elders. And they don't know me."

"You won't be alone. Tish may be going, too," said Nora, her green eyes flashing gold.

"But she's only fourteen," said Adam. He liked the idea of seeing Tish again, and the idea of being with her for a while made him happy, but this was adult work and Tish was even younger than he was.

"Almost fifteen, and she's also quite bright and observant. And strong. You know how strong and brave she is. Besides, Blanchfleur wants her there. Our whole group trusts both of you, and we all agree that you'd be more than acceptable representatives, who will not intimidate the more conservative elders of the forest people," said Nora.

"And Kate, the chief, will be bringing her son, Paul, and some others of the First Nation youth to the meetings. Kate put the idea of involving the youth to the elders, and they were quite pleased to be doing this. Sometimes there are advantages to being young.

"But there is one other thing I'll tell you first before I let the others know. When I met with them they warned me of a threat to our well-being, outsiders and forest people alike," continued Mabon.

"A threat?" Adam asked, his chin pushed forward as it did when he was curious or perplexed. "What kind of threat? Are we in danger now?"

"Perhaps. Sometime before long. Some of us. Especially the little ones," Mabon said, his forehead wrinkling.

Mabon, the powerful former forest Ranger, was beginning to show signs of getting older. Yet he remained, especially in the eyes of Adam and Nora, the same large and powerful adult who had protected them and made them feel safe. But there was no denying the fact that his hair was dotted with grey and wrinkles were forming around his bright blue eyes and on his tanned forehead. These clear eyes were narrowed and serious now, as they often were when he spoke of important matters.

"Raiders have been trying to kidnap children and babies from relatives and neighbours south of the People of the Forest," he said.

"Babies," said Adam. "Like Nora stole me away from the city?" He frowned.

"No," said Mabon. "They're not trying to save these children the way Nora saved you from the city." Indeed she had; he had been slated to be terminated. She had saved Adam's life.

"Who is trying to do this kidnapping and why?" asked Adam, his curiosity fully aroused.

"No one knows. But the gossip among the forest people is that babies are being kidnapped by armed raiders. They're entering the villages in the dark of night and stealing the little children away."

"That's terrible," said Adam. "Raiders?" He remembered Blanchfleur's knights, who raided the happy valley and destroyed his beloved old ones.

"Yes," said Mabon. The big man put his huge hands on his son's solid shoulders, squeezed them firmly, and looked intently into his brown eyes. "Will you think seriously about what I've asked you?"

"What did Tish say?" asked Adam, his heart pounding.

"She said she would if you would."

"I'll think about it," said Adam, his cheerful voice betraying more than a passing interest in the idea of sharing this duty with Tish, Alice's daughter.

"There's one other thing I was to tell you," said Mabon. "One very important thing."

"What?" said Adam.

"If you or anyone else is threatened by these raiders I mentioned, run with whoever is near you as deeply into the woods as you need to go to feel safe, and then hide. Stay there and remain as still as possible for two days before you come out. When you do, be careful and do not go directly back to our village, but gather quietly beside the large oak where you and I used to sit and watch the stars together. Do you remember the place? It has changed. The trees and plants have grown."

"Tish and I went there just days ago. I wanted to show her where you and I used to go."

"What should you do?" Mabon asked.

"Run and hide," he said, "and stay out of sight for two days and then wait for help near our special large oak. But we're not babies or little children, are we?"

"No, but we can't be too careful," said Mabon. "I have a feeling in my gut that I don't like. Now remember. Just in case. Be ready. Even if we never have to use our special meeting place, we'll both know a safe place to go if we ever get separated for any reason."

Chapter 2:
The Lost Ones

"So how long have we been walking this time?" asked Elroy. Elroy was a large man who had been overweight the day they left the Manuhome on the underground trains that Doctor Ueland had built as an emergency escape hatch for his workers. Some of the boys in the home had called Elroy "fat boy," but they kept their distance when they did; he was as strong and dangerous as an angry bear.

That was many months ago and Elroy was no longer quite so fat. The wild had seen to that. He had had his fill of the wild. His denim work clothes were well worn and pitted with rips and tears. They now hung more loosely on his huge, muscular frame.

"Long time," said Hen. He was small with fiery red hair that he kept greased in a peak like a rooster's comb and an equally red face. His real name was Henry, and he didn't like to be called Hen, but he was so much smaller than his two angry companions that he did not dare say so to either of them.

"How long, Mack?" repeated Elroy, as he shook his head and sneered at Henry. "Is this the third or the fourth year since the explosions at the Manuhome?"

Mack coughed and spat out the bitter spruce gum he had been chewing. He reached into his backpack and took out the small bundle of counting sticks he kept tied together in there and moved the sticks around, counting aloud as he went. He finished, spat again, and said, "It's been about three years."

"Are we going back in there tonight?" asked Hen. "I don't think we should be doing this."

Mack spat on the ground one more time. He made Hen squirm as he thought up how to respond to the little guy. Mack was not as tall as Elroy, but it was clear to anyone who met this trio of lost souls which one was in charge.

"Are you assuming you have any choice in where we go or what we do?" he asked. "We agreed to follow Moses, and I am not letting any of you off the hook. Can you see any other way for us to have any sort of a future?"

One day last year they had stopped at what remained of an abandoned farm property. Mack had ransacked the remaining dilapidated building and discovered a large metal storage locker in the sealed closet of a cramped space where someone had once been living, in the upper level of what had once clearly been a barn with stalls for a number of animals. They had managed to break the lock, and inside the locker they had found a carefully folded khaki military uniform that someone must have mothballed following a battle in one of the many wars of the past.

The jacket and trousers fit Mack perfectly after both Elroy and Hen had attempted trying it on. Mack had begun wearing it, along with a pair of fine leather boots that were the envy of everyone they had met since then. Mack, with his tanned, leathery skin and his bright blue eyes, made an impressive figure in the old officer's outfit. Mack had said he looked like a general he had seen in a book, but nobody else knew exactly what a general was.

There had also been a few medals still in their cases in a decorated leather pouch, and Mack had pinned these across the khaki on his chest. Mack had hard, muscular arms from his years in the metal fabrication shops of the Manuhome. They had found a woollen beret with a brass pin and a broken feather in the locker, but the beret was much too small for Mack's large head. Mack didn't care for hats anyway, and he had been glad to leave it behind in the old locker. And then they had left, but not before they burned the barn to the ground. The burning of the tinder-dry building was the best part of their day. They whooped and hollered until the intense heat and the rain of sparks became too hot to bear. They were happy to find a sleeping place under a tall oak in the nearby cool grass and sleep, contented that their day had brought them so much fun and entertainment.

The next morning, they came to the shore of a large lake and decided to follow northward close beside its banks until they discovered a clearing on the edge of the forest, where they spotted the rusting wreckage of a giant helicopter and rusted piles of metal they realized were the remains of robots and killbots Mack had probably helped to construct at the Manuhome several years ago.

They looked over the old parts and tried to figure out if anything was worth salvaging, but with no tools or computers, and the likelihood that there were no satellites overhead, they realized all they had found was worthless junk.

It was time to continue their journey in search of innocents they could capture and take away, child by child, little children to help them establish a new community for themselves from the

Indigenous families and runaways they had been told were hiding in this part of the wild. This, Moses said, was the only way to add to the population of the many doomed escaped workers from the Manuhome, who could have no children themselves thanks to the actions of their Insider managers, who had only kept them alive for their labour. All Manuhome workers had been neutered before being transferred to Doctor Ueland at the Manuhome to work as slaves until they were no longer needed. If they didn't take children to raise themselves, their freedom would become meaningless; the group couldn't survive more than a few more decades.

Now, after only a few weeks of difficult travel through rough territory, they had discovered what Moses, their young and determined leader, had sent them to find. There were, it seemed, many unauthorized people living in the forest—men, women, and children all living together as families. Eating and sleeping and having babies. The three lost ones had found part of the answer to the dreams of Moses. They had only to take back what the insiders had denied them, a few healthy children and babies who they could raise as their own families to insure their futures as human beings.

Their first and only foray into the night had ended in failure. As they walked amid the huts and tents of a sleepy, prosperous village, they had been spotted by a small yappy dog. The people woke up, armed themselves with rocks, clubs, and spears, and the trio had been fortunate to escape with their lives.

The small baby Hen had stolen yelled so much that Hen got frightened and set it down beside a narrow stream. Hen thought he would have been captured and perhaps murdered by the forest dwellers if the large young man pursuing him hadn't stopped to tend to the screaming child.

Hen had been pleased that the child had managed to cry out and distract his pursuer. The three raiders decided to wait a day or two before entering any of the nearby villages again and make another attempt to carry out Moses's wishes.

Chapter 3:
About the Raiders

When Adam awoke from the nightmare, he was pleased and surprised to see Nora sitting on the ground beside his blanket roll and sleeping skins. The bad dream had been frightening. In it someone had loudly called out "Run, run!" and Adam had gotten out from under his skins and had run off into the forest. He had gone to the special meeting place that Mabon had reminded him about at their last meeting. He waited and waited, yet no one came.

All around him he had heard human voices and animal voices calling out in fear and panic. He sat up now, relieved that his frightening memories had been a dream but still feeling the aftermath of fright. Nora, his mother, opened her arms, inviting a hug, something she used to do most every morning when he was a boy back in the hidden valley with Mabon and the old ones. She smiled as if to say, "Come on, aren't you glad to see me?"

He was more than glad, and so he joined with her in a comforting hug which, as his heart rate lowered, went on much longer than a fifteen-year-old forest dweller was normally comfortable with. And yet he felt wonderful to have her back home.

"How was the latest meeting with all those elders? It must have been great to hear from all those other tribes," he said. "I am so proud that you were picked to represent all of us on council."

"It was interesting," Nora answered. Her face appeared drawn, as if she hadn't eaten or slept well; she looked tired and worried.

"Mom," Adam asked, "what is a raider? Do you mean people like the knights that Blanchfleur sent into the Happy Valley to attack old ones?" Adam felt funny discussing the bloody attack launched by Blanchfleur, Tish's grandmother, because so many things had changed since then. Like the way that she and Doctor Ueland had saved them all. The night the satellites fell had begun many happy months of peace, with no signs of danger until now.

"Who told you about the raiders?" she asked.

"Mabon," Adam said. "And he told me what we should do if we were attacked."

"Oh, I see. So, the rumours must have gotten here while I was away at the discussions," she said.

"What rumours? Were they about the raiders?"

His mother didn't answer right away. "Where is Mabon?" she asked.

"Are you going to tell me?" Adam asked, his voice anxious, his eyes wide with curiosity.

"I'll tell you what I know. And it is just based on the speculation of the council and some things you and Blanchfleur's father told me."

"Doctor Ueland?" said Adam.

"Yes," she said, her eyebrows lowered as she always did when the doctor's name was mentioned. Adam missed the former manager of the Manuhome too; the brilliant doctor had saved his life more than once, and he'd sacrificed his own life, not only for Adam and his mother, but for so many others.

"Tell me, then…please," he said.

"Just an angry and frightened group of people," she said. "They are unfortunate human beings who see themselves as having no future, no home, no place to live. "Raiders" in this case is just a stupid nickname. These raiders are what remains of a handful of the surviving people who did manufacturing and agricultural work for the insiders, the residents of Aahimsa."

"So, you mean the Manuhome workers. What about them? Most of them died in the attack over three years ago," he said.

"Yes, most of them," she said. "Do you remember anything from the day you and Doctor Ueland escaped from the Manuhome and came to rescue Blanchfleur, Alice, and Tish?"

"Of course I do. Go on," he said.

"Blanchfleur's father told us as we escaped by train that many of the workers escaped the blast and headed south on two underground trains, in tunnels he had built." Nora watched her boy's intense interest. "It seems," she said, "Alice told me once that the insiders who knew of the homelands named the Manuhome workers 'worker bees,' and ironically that is how the insider kill bots referred to them as they did their hunt. Blanchfleur said that her father, Doctor Ueland, mentioned the fact as he lay dying the night the stars fell."

Adam remembered how happy they were as the satellites tumbled to earth from the sky that night like a thousand falling stars, and how sad they were to hear of Ueland's death when the badly hurt Blanchfleur came back to their camp more than three years ago. "But why were they called 'worker bees'?"

"I can only guess. Worker bees work. They are sterile. The queen and the drones are female and male. So these people who can't have families did all the manual and intellectual labour at the Manuhome".

"Why are we in danger now?" Adam asked.

"It would appear that a significant number of the workers are still alive, and, after a brief and discouraging search for new lives in the south, they've come back up north. The confederacy of tribal councils is sure they are the ones who have been accused of taking young children and babies from forest people down along the coast." Nora's voice had quieted to a whisper as she ended the sentence. Her green eyes were now shining with tears.

"But why?" asked Adam.

"I don't know," his mother said. "Nobody seems to know, but everyone is brokenhearted and frightened." She took Adam into her arms again and they stayed like that until they heard Mabon's footsteps approach the sleeping shelter.

Chapter 4:
Guns

Early the next day, Adam was excited to hear that Tish had agreed to join him as the second youth representative on the elders' upcoming council meeting.

"You will both be asked to speak on any topic. Neither of you will have a vote. Only the tribal elders and the chiefs have a vote. But everyone who is present and invited there has a right to be heard," said Mabon, "and your voice will be listened to and acted upon."

"I doubt they care what a kid has to say," said Adam.

"The tribal council listens to the people, all who have been invited to live in peace alongside the forest people. Age doesn't matter, and everyone is equal. Learning is the important matter. Male and female alike of any age, all equal," said Nora.

"So, neither you nor Mabon will be going with us?" said Adam. "You're sure that's wise?"

"We're not going this time. Blanchfleur has offered to take you as far as the river bend, where you will be meeting several of the elders who will travel to the meeting place with you. You and Tish are to bring your bows and a quiver of arrows, your best knife, your medicine bag, and a supply of berries and nuts and some dried meat. Your hosts will be feeding you after the council meeting, and you will spend the night in their camp before heading back home. Blanchfleur, or one of us, will meet you at the river bend on the way home. I hope you'll be careful and listen to what the elders tell you. There are new dangers," said Mabon.

"You mean the worker bees?"

"Yes, I think so. The vanished workers who escaped capture and are suspected of carrying out the raids on the villages. And there have been rumours of raids farther to the south of here. Raids where children and women have been taken away by strangers carrying guns."

"Did any of the forest people have guns?" asked Nora.

"The forest people have agreed to not use them," said Mabon. "Guns only make things worse. We know how the world was long ago and could be again. We must try to keep life simple and learn to live in peace together. There must be no guns, no weapons of any kind to be used in battle, if possible. We must find a better way. That's why when you travel to the council meeting you will move slowly and silently. If we armed ourselves with guns, others would find more and better guns, and on and on it would go like it was before, and we know how that ended: the near end of all human life on the planet."

"Where did the raiders' guns come from?" asked Nora.

"Who knows? They may have found old guns and ammunition somewhere. The world's garbage heaps are still littered with lost, hidden, and broken things, and a few unhappy and broken people still remain here and there among us," said Mabon.

"Why were there guns, anyway?" asked Adam.

"Long ago, people hunted for their food with weapons they invented and produced themselves—spears, bows, and arrows like we made for ourselves in the Hidden Valley for the protection of the old ones. And at times like that, they were used as weapons in fights to protect homes and families. People invented explosives and guns and cannons and then nuclear missiles and long-range rockets, and powerful drones, and on and on, until they destroyed cities and countries and nearly destroyed the planet.

"Rich people and investors and countries made so much money from selling guns or from making weapons, or making money by lending it to people who paid them interest from the money they made from making and selling them. They sold to one group and then to the enemies of that group, then built more powerful guns and weapons," said Mabon. "The more wars, the more money rich people made, and the more suffering the poor and the innocent were forced to endure."

"So sad," said Adam. His eyes were wet and red, and he forced himself to look away from Mabon. "I'm sorry," he said to his father.

"I'm glad you understand and have feelings for those who suffer," said the large man, as he drew Adam to him and held him tight in his fierce, comforting grip. They stayed like that a few moments, and Mabon continued. "There is danger, and we must not let it get out of hand."

Mabon and Adam joined Nora, who also embraced her son and spoke. "So be careful and look after Tish and the elders. And come home to us safe," she said. Then it was a three-way embrace, including their whole family.

In another camp across the small lake, the golden-haired Tish lived with her mother, Alice, and her once powerful grandmother, Blanchfleur, the former mayor of the lost city of Aahimsa, now fully recovered from her injuries in her battle against the kill bots on the night of the falling stars. Blanchfleur had battled alongside Doctor Ueland, her father, the masterful commander of Aahimsa's Manufacturing Homeland, who had died in that battle to save them all, battling alongside annoying Gloria, one-time enemy and latter-day hero. Since that day, the former mayor lived a life free of politics and difficult decisions, surrounded by her loving family and abundant new friends.

Shortly after their arrival in the forest, Alice had decided that it would be easier for all of them if she and Nora didn't share the same community village day after day, although everyone else was content that all the old enemies should be reconciled to sharing the same fires and the same village.

Alice and family tried for a while but had bowed out and left after a few months. Tish went along reluctantly Blanchfleur and her, saying something like "blood is thicker than water." She missed her original family too much to stay separated from them. But from the start the two families remained good neighbours and managed a high degree of friendship and contentment as they settled into their separate camps. The lake was quite small, and quickly crossed, and the two camps quickly became one village circling a small, shared lake.

Tish found, to her great surprise, that as she grew and matured here in this natural place, far away from the city she had known, she greatly missed the rather brief but intense moments of excitement she had shared with Adam during their escape from Aahimsa and area. Adam would always remain the Wild Boy to her, no matter how much she came to admire and enjoy his company. There were gatherings several times a year where the villages got together for fishing and food preparation, and for games and celebrations, and somehow the youngsters always gravitated together, and their friendship continued to grow as much during their absences as in these planned, regular encounters.

She had been as surprised and delighted as Adam had been by the offer from the tribal council that she and Adam together represent their village at meetings, and she had been given a similar set of instructions, including the suggestion she should look after Adam and the elders. She was also delighted by how excited she felt at the prospect of accompanying her old "enemy" on this outing with the tribal elders. She would heed the advice and try to keep quiet and to move slowly. She had no experience in dealing with kidnappers or with raiders armed with guns. And she had no interest in gaining any such experience.

Chapter 5: Kidnapped

Blanchfleur had left the two young people temporarily in the company of the elders to go to a nearby spring to refill water skins. She suggested Adam and Tish stay back, well out of sight, until her return. She would bring them fresh drinking water and stay close to them until their escorts from the forest people's village arrived. She had been gone a very short time when Adam whispered to Tish.

"I heard something," he said, his upright finger poised in front of his lips.

Tish nodded and the elders stopped talking and eased closer around the boy, their eyes darting nervously from left to right. Adam prepared himself for the worst, planning how he could be of most use to Tish and the elders.

"What exactly did you hear?" Tish asked. All faces turned to Adam, who signalled to them once again, with a raised finger still before his lips, to remain silent. "Shush," he whispered. He turned to Tish. "A twig snapped, leaves rustling."

He signalled again for silence and pointed to the ground. The others dropped to their knees and crouched close to the sweet-smelling forest floor. The ferns around them stood fully erect and Tish found a cool frond tickling her nose. She too struggled to keep from sneezing. Suddenly she felt a rough burlap bag being pulled over her head, causing her to cough from its rank odour and dryness. She was yanked backwards and tried to cry out, but a large and powerful hand quickly covered her mouth and cut off all but a whimper of terror and despair.

Adam rushed to her aid but was knocked to the ground by the solid butt of a hunting rifle slammed against his skull. A deep voice warned the frightened elders, "Don't you move a muscle. My gun is loaded, and I'm not scared to use it." It was the last thing Adam heard before something hit him hard again. As he passed out, he, too, was aware of the rough, foul-smelling cloth around his head and he was lifted and carried quickly away from the meeting place.

When Blanchfleur returned several minutes later laden with bulging water skins, she found only the forlorn group of worried elders huddled together close to the trees. The elderly and frail forest dwellers excitedly explained as best they could what had happened and warned her that there were at least three large intruders and one had a loaded hunting rifle. They also said they had sent one of their members to their village to bring back help.

Blanchfleur immediately prepared to head off in the direction the elders indicated the kidnappers had taken. She snatched a couple of water bags and left behind the rest for the elders to share. She grabbed Adam's bow and as many arrows as she could carry. She checked to see if her knife was in its scabbard and she turned to the frightened elders.

"Stay put until the escort comes for you. I'm going after the youngsters. Ask them to send someone to our village and have them send others out to help me find these monsters. If I can find enough signs, I will follow them to the ends of the earth if necessary. I will mark my journey by breaking branches, bending grasses, and drawing arrows on bare patches of ground. Tell them to bring one or more trackers, a strong tracker, and as I asked, perhaps one or more of you can send someone or return to our villages and let Mabon, Nora, Alice, and the councils of the forest people know that we need help. Good luck. I must move fast while I still have enough light to track them."

When she next squatted near the river to fill her water skins, she had had time to look around and take in the forest sounds, the wind in the abundant leaves, now fully unfurled, and hear the hum of the busy insects and the hundreds of birdsongs. She felt a sense of well-being, and she was optimistic about finding her youngsters. She was, at the same time, angry and determined. These nasty barbarians should be easy to follow. They were not likely accustomed to these woods or to any wilderness, for that matter.

These past few years had been years of abundance, of friendships, of sharing with their new families: the forest people, as they called themselves. At first, she and her family and her fellow travellers, her former enemies and opponents, had assumed that the forest people were mostly the descendants of the Indigenous peoples who had occupied these lands for thousands upon thousands of years.

Instead, they discovered that while many could trace their ancestors back almost forever, it seemed that many others were descended from persons who had somehow escaped the upheavals of the new order and had slipped into the forest and found ways to survive, largely thanks to the knowledge and the guidance of the few Indigenous elders who had managed to live through generation after generation of neglect and abuse by countless land-hungry arrivals from various European "civilizations."

At first the elders cautiously trusted the trickle of immigrants into their forests. They helped the lost and helpless runaways when necessary, and they taught them how to survive and to thrive without the so-called "necessities" of the mad world they had left behind. Gradually, the arrivals who chose to stay discovered that those "necessities and luxuries" had been the real masters of their lives and popular "smart" devices had been herding them into an electronic form of apathy and slavery. The people of the forest began to mix and blend, shared talents and secrets and knowledge, and chose to discard ideas and attachments to things that separated them from the forest and all blessings that life on earth contained and nourished.

Many of those years they had been bound together out of necessity, as they were hunted intermittently. They never knew when they would be discovered by an overhead spy satellite or a flyover by armed drones and kill bots. They had been poisoned from above, their forests bombed and destroyed. But, somehow, many had survived and learned ways to stay out of sight, to be virtually invisible.

All that had changed on the night of the falling stars, the night that Blanchfleur and her father, Doctor Ueland, had silenced these threats by disabling the entire world's satellite control and communication system. It was no longer necessary to hide. They were free to enjoy every aspect of their forest existence, including a clear, open sky and full sunshine, beyond the constant cover of the forest dome.

All these thoughts filled Blanchfleur's mind as she sought every visible sign of the kidnapper's passage. She found scuffed earth regularly where the young people had been dragged along. Then there had been other signs, hundreds of them, thousands of bruised and broken plants, bent grasses, twisted stems, heel marks, and more. These were people who knew nothing of the forest, and who had no affinity for the natural world. "They're barbarians," she muttered.

As daylight dimmed to twilight and then settled into darkness, she wondered how far ahead the kidnappers had gotten. She finally decided to stop for the night on the top of a steep grassy hill whose crest was covered in small coarse bushes which had seasonally occupied it for years and prevented taller trees from flourishing. She couldn't expect protection from the wind up so high, but she would be able to see the countryside for miles around.

For a few hours, she sat in darkness as clouds
buried stars and moon. Though she was exhausted
and growing drowsy, she waited, and eventually was
rewarded with a small glow in the gloomy distance
that soon grew into a substantial blaze. She marked
the direction by drawing a long arrow on a patch
of sandy ground that had been claimed as home
by black ants. Then she wrapped herself in a heavy
blanket and quickly stole some much-needed rest.

Chapter 6: Around the Fire

Blanchfleur woke as the first signs of morning began to reveal the outlines of trees and define the clouds overhead. Already a chorus of songbirds and patrols of shouting crows had begun to cheerily herald the coming day. The injuries she had suffered at the hands of the kill bots had not been much of a bother recently, but a variety of scars and aging joints were not happy with her dozing on the cold, rocky ground. She yawned and then forced herself to slowly stand and stretch.

She stepped over to reexamine the arrow she had scratched on the bare patch of ground last night at the hill's edge. She stared off into the direction indicated. The landscape looked much different as light and shadow began to take their firm hold on the shape of morning. She thought she detected a few out-of-place wisps of smoke rising above a particularly tall white spruce to her west. She selected a path she could follow where the spruce would remain visible, and she hurried off as quickly as a slight limp and regular jolts of minor pain would allow.

Before long she was certain she had come close to where she had seen the smoke and fire, and she knew to be cautious. The kidnappers might have set out a sentry, though she doubted they would think it necessary to do so.

She moved a few careful yards and stopped to listen before taking the next step. Before long she detected the regular bass snorts of some creature snoring, likely a human creature to be sleeping so late, one of her prey. Now she moved tree by tree, careful to avoid fallen twigs and leaves, dry branches, and patches of long, dry, tangled grass that might signal her presence to an alert sentry. At last she was able to detect at least one sleeping form—that of a large man who, according to the regular rise of his gut, appeared perhaps to be the source of the snoring. Lying close to him, tied firmly to the trunk of the same huge pine she had used as a guidepost, their backs to the trunk on opposite sides of it, sat the two well-loved youngsters she had been seeking.

They seemed to be sleeping, but it was difficult to tell, as they appeared to be gagged as well as tied up in heavy ropes. Blanchfleur was tired and sore, and as it would be foolhardy to confront the captors alone, she settled down and rested against a small poplar hidden among the skirts of a ring of tangled spruce.

All along the morning's trek she had managed to leave exaggerated signs of her passage. She was sure that Mabon, Nora, Alice, and some of the other forest people would be able to follow with ease and soon find them, whether they were those in her own villages or the villages and settlements of the many other council members.

She could smell the dewy, dark remains of the smoldering wood fire and the roasted food they had been cooking. She was even more acutely aware of the growling of her empty stomach. The rumbling of her insides seemed loud to her, but she doubted it would carry far enough to be heard by her prey or the youngsters.

She sat quietly amid the familiar, comforting sounds of the forest and was beginning to nod off again when she heard faint, familiar voices coming from the nearby camp.

"Can you hear me?" the first voice whispered. Her granddaughter, Tish. After a short pause, she heard Adam's reply in a soft and tentative whisper. Obviously they were far enough away from their captors, or the captors were still sleeping, although whoever had been snoring had suddenly stopped.

Blanchfleur crouched in the now silent forest, listening for the next voice.

"Are you okay?" Adam asked, finally. "Did they hurt you?"

"Yes, and no," she whispered, speaking even more softly, taking her cue from Adam's muted tone.

"Can you see them?" he asked. "I can't."

"Sort of," she replied. "They sent one guy away, the little one with the crazy red hair."

"Hen," said Adam.

"Yes, I think so," she agreed. "It was Hen."

"Why did they send him?" asked Adam. "I must have been asleep. I didn't hear anything. I was worried about you and all I could see was the dark trees all around me. Why did they send Hen away?"

"I heard them say 'Moses.' I'm pretty sure that was it. The tanned guy in the old uniform, with the blue eyes, I think he is in charge here, but he isn't the boss. I heard him say, 'Go and get Moses and maybe some of the others. Tell him we found some babies. Lots of them,'" said Tish. Her voice sounded curious. Blanchfleur could tell that she was perplexed.

"Babies?" said Adam. "Then why did they take us? We're not babies."

"I don't know...I wonder who this Moses is. You did say Moses, didn't you?"

The conversation was interrupted by a loud, authoritative voice; one of the sleeping figures had awoken. "Shut up, you two!" said the voice. "No talking or you'll be sorry. You'll get lots of chances to talk once the others get here."

That must be the tanned guy, thought Blanchfleur, *the one who Tish said was the boss here.*

"You want me to shut them up?" said another gruff voice.

"No, Fat Boy. I don't think that will be necessary," said the tanned guy voice. "They'll be quiet if they're as smart as I think they are. Get ready to move back to our other camp."

Chapter 7:
All for One

It was well after dark when the elder spoke to Mabon and Nora. Mabon was prepared to set out at once in search of the youngsters and their captors. Nora pointed out the difficulties of finding signs of the travellers in the dark, and morning light was still hours away. She convinced him that they should cross the lake by canoe and speak to Alice before they left. Tish was Alice's daughter and Blanchfleur was Alice's mother and Alice certainly had to be filled in on what was going on.

"Hurry, then," said her powerful and impatient companion as he dragged the canoe across the sandy bank till it floated on the edge of the small lake.

"You go," Nora said. "I'll gather up a few of our things and a bit of food and blankets. We have no way of knowing how long we'll be gone."

Mabon nodded and jumped into the sleek birch-bark canoe, which was underway before Nora had time to turn around and hurry back to their lodge.

\\

Alice was sleeping soundly, and when she awoke and saw someone standing in silhouette inside her door, she let out a frightened yelp. But when she heard Mabon's kindly voice and the reason he had come, she insisted on gathering a few things for herself and Tish, and a few of her mother's warmer bits of clothing. Soon they had crossed the lake a second time and were unloading their things. Nora arrived with her parcels and Mabon's precious medicine bag and together they set out in silence.

They made their way to the crossing, and with the remaining moonlight were able to travel about a kilometre before heavy cloud erased their light. They quickly set up a makeshift camp where they would try to rest until daylight dawned in a few short hours.

In the morning Nora was the first to wake. She refilled their water skins from a nearby stream and arrived back just as Mabon and Alice were preparing a meagre breakfast of crusty bread and goat cheese from their limited stores. Then they set out once again, Mabon in the lead, as he rapidly found the many signs that the unwitting kidnappers had left, and the excellent, even more obvious ones he recognized as having been left intentionally by Blanchfleur.

Half an hour later, they found the nearly cooled ashes and charred bits of wood of the kidnappers' camp. There was no sign of Adam or Tish or of their captors, or of Blanchfleur.

"Do you think they're all right?" said Alice, her face betraying her worst fears.

"I'm not too concerned at the moment," said Mabon as he looked over the camp with practiced eyes. "There's been no sign of a struggle, or any kind of violence. Look here," he said, squatting beside the base of a large pine tree. He pointed to abrasions that circled the old hardwood trunk.

"I'd say that the youngsters were tied up here," Mabon said. "And so, I'd guess, they don't know that Blanchfleur is close behind them. That's good, because they won't be feeling the need to be in any special hurry."

"How far do you think they've gone?" asked Alice. "Why did they take our kids, anyway? What could they want?"

"I have no idea," said Nora. "What do you think, Mabon?"

"I don't know, but I can imagine lots of possibilities," he said. He paused and quickly made his decision. "Later, we can talk. I suggest that that we only speak when necessary and when we do, we keep our voices low. Right now, we should be trying to make up valuable time, and we don't want them to have a clue that we're anywhere close."

Chapter 8: Blanchfleur

Blanchfleur had heard the approach of Nora, Mabon, Alice, and Tish. They were following a narrow path close off to the left beside her now. She wanted to call out to them and warn them they were already too close to the kidnappers for anyone's comfort and safety, but she knew any communication could be heard by the outlaw group. Serious harm might come to Tish and Adam.

Instead, she decided to take a chance on stepping quietly out of her hiding place, with her hands held high, hoping she could give them a sign to remain as quiet as possible.

She took a quick breath and leapt out close to Nora, who was startled and let out an involuntary peep of fright. Mabon quickly caught hold of her. He covered his loved one's mouth gently with his large hand. The others heard the rustle of leaves and the brief, bird-like sound, and, though surprised to see Blanchfleur, they quietly approached and embraced her while she, her first finger upright before her lips, signalled for silence and tried to indicate that the kidnappers and the two youngsters were just a few dozen metres off to their right.

"I have a plan," she whispered into Nora's ear. Mabon heard and signalled his willingness to get the plan into action. Blanchfleur pointed at the ground and immediately sat. She motioned for all to gather near her. She held up her right hand with four fingers raised.

"We'll go in together, Mabon and I," said Nora. She looked at Mabon to see his response. He merely waited. "We'll move slowly from opposite sides. We'll free the kids if we can do it safely. But do nothing until we're in there together. This is how we've stayed alive for a long time. We'll be careful to not place the children in greater danger than they already find themselves in."

Blanchfleur looked worried, but she nodded. "Do you want me to come with you?" she asked.

"If you wish. But it might be best if you stayed behind, ready to go for more help if anything unexpected happens," said Nora. Blanchfleur glanced at Mabon, who nodded his agreement.

"All right," said Blanchfleur, her voice disappointed. "I'll lie low and wait."

Nora looked up at the sky, where a small cloud partially covered a nearly full moon. "I'll head west and then go south a short way. You go east and then south. I'll see you soon. We'll skirt their camp from both sides and look for anyone awake or on watch. If we can get to the kids, we'll move together and get them out of there. Then we'll return and gather these goons up to take back to camp for questioning. How does that sound?" she asked.

Mabon smiled and then spoke softly as he gave her a short, reassuring hug. "Let's do it," he said.

Chapter 9: Hen's Journey

At first Hen thought Moses had moved camp while he and Elroy and Mack were away, but when he came to a ridge he hadn't seen before and looked up at the bright half-moon, he realized he was lost, having travelled too far north. He would backtrack a bit and then head south again and watch for the small river that ran by their old camp.

After an hour of stumbling through thick brush, he came to the river and recognized a couple of landmarks along its bank. He knew where he was standing, and he soon saw the glow of a large campfire. He recognized Moses, who stood near the fire despite his heavy, dark woollen cloak. He wasn't holding his usual leather Bible but was addressing a handful of his loyal followers.

When the listeners noticed Hen's approach,

Moses stopped speaking, and he and several others left their circle and came over to greet their red-headed friend.

"How are you and the others?" asked Moses. "Do you bring good news or bad? You haven't heard of any marauders, have you?"

"Good news, I think. We have found lots of children and other people. Lots of them," said Hen. He tried to remember if there was anything else. "I think Mack wants some of you to come back to help us."

"I see," said Moses. "Lots of them. Hm…"

"Lots," said Hen.

"And, Henry," he said, his voice slow and measured, the way he spoke when he had already guessed the answer, "tell me you didn't run into trouble. You didn't meet any angry workers? We've heard from some of our other seekers that a few marauders have been ruining things for us. They are damaging villages and hurting innocent people. The people and the babies…" He paused and looked Henry hard in the eyes. Henry felt suddenly afraid.

"I'm sorry," he said, his eyes on the stony ground.

"What do you mean?" said Moses, his voice angry and disturbed. "It wasn't you, was it?"

"I didn't mean to," said Hen.

"Didn't mean to what?" asked Moses, his usually

kind face turning red as the nearby blaze, his eyes shining with anger.

"A dog woke up and lots of angry people chased me and the others. I had to put down the baby and run."

"Did you harm the child?" asked Moses, his voice still loud and threatening. "Did you hurt people and burn the village?"

"No, no," Hen said, terrified. "We ran away."

"What else did you do?" asked Moses, still annoyed.

"Later on, we took a big boy and a girl," Hen said, his voice quiet and nervous.

"Did anyone see you?" asked Moses.

"Yes," the redhead answered.

"And what happened then?"

"Nothing, we have them at our camp. Mack wants you to come. There are lots more of them. Lots."

Chapter 10: In the enemy's camp

Nora came near to the two sleeping figures next to the small wood fire which, though burning low, still gave off enough glow that with the sky full of stars, and the half-moon out of the few wispy clouds, she could see that they were both sleeping, not just the one who was snoring. She moved quietly through the tall ferns, well out of the meagre light from the fire, and swung up toward the tall tree where she could make out the familiar figure of Mabon kneeling at its wide base.

She watched, as she carefully approached, Mabon place a large hand over Adam's mouth and saw their wild boy instantly relax as he recognized the powerful man who had brought him up, the former Ranger who had saved his life over and over. Mabon untied the clumsy knots that held Adam to one side of the tree as Nora gently woke Tish, also covering her mouth to prevent her crying out and alerting the sleeping kidnappers.

The youngsters were elated at being set free and could hardly control their joy. The foursome made their way back to Blanchfleur, the kids beside Nora. Mabon gathered up the rope and the strips of cloth he assumed had been intended to gag Adam and Tish then turned toward the sleeping kidnappers.

"Come with us," whispered Nora aloud, but Mabon signalled for silence and shook his head. The three others headed back to where Blanchfleur anxiously awaited their return.

When they arrived, there was silent celebration and grins of happiness as they waited for the arrival of their constant companion, champion, and help-mate. The moments dragged on until they heard someone or something large and awkward making its way noisily through the trees. They moved back as far as they could get into the shadows and a mas-sive figure appeared and dropped its heavy burden to the ground.

"Sorry I startled you," said Mabon. "This one is quite a load even for me, and he really needs a bath. Keep an eye on him while I go back for the mouthy guy. He's not too happy at being trussed up, but he had better settle down or he may have to be rattled a bit. When I get back, we'll try and find an easier way to get them moving with us. I want to be out of here before somebody else comes along and finds us here. This one kept saying that others were coming. He pulled a rifle on me, but I took it and it wasn't loaded anyway. I smashed it against a tree and twisted the barrel. I left it in the nearby woods. It won't be hurting or scaring anybody else."

A very few minutes later, two figures appeared, one in old military attire with tall, shiny boots of dark leather. He appeared to be calm and under control, even with his hands tied behind him and Mabon at his side holding a thick rope that encircled his prisoner's solid neck. The captive man stood silently and waited after giving his trussed companion an almost amused look.

Mabon knelt beside the large man on the ground and spoke in a kindly voice. "Do I have to carry you the rest of the way or would you rather walk with us?"

The standing figure spoke then said, "What are you going to do with us?"

"That depends on you," he said. "We have to talk with you and find out what you are doing around here. Then we'll have to decide as a group what will happen. We are probably not going to harm you. But we can't have you kidnapping our young people. What are your names and where are you from?"

"They call me Mack, and that one is Elroy," said the tall man.

"Are you a real soldier?" asked Adam, who had been listening in silence with Tish and Nora.

Mack laughed. "No. I found this outfit a few weeks back and it was better than what I was wearing. So I took it. I used to work in the Manuhome. I was an engineer in the metal fabrication shop. You wouldn't believe the things I designed along with Ueland's other scientists and designers."

Adam recalled the happy times he had spent with Doctor Ueland, but Tish interrupted his thoughts. "We should get out of here."

"I agree," said Mack, sensing an opportunity. "Get Elroy on his feet and he'll walk along with us peacefully," he said. "We'd just as soon be out of here before the others come."

"Why is that?" asked Nora.

"Let's leave it for now," suggested Adam. "I'd rather be away from here too."

"Me too," agreed Tish.

"Sounds wise," said Nora.

By now Mabon had untied Elroy's feet, and the heavy man had, with the former Ranger's help, gotten shakily to his feet.

"You don't need to tie our hands. We'll go willingly and be happy to talk with you, if we can get far enough away from Moses and his gang," said Mack.

"We'll keep your hands tied until we get closer to home. But if you behave you'll be untied real soon," said Mabon.

Elroy was silent through all of this. He wondered if Mack knew what he was doing. Elroy wasn't so sure he wanted to get on the bad side of Moses and his black leather book. "I'll settle for that. Come on, Elroy, behave yourself. These are good people and I don't want anything more to do with Moses and his crew. They've already almost ruined everything."

Nora led the way and the two youngsters followed her. Next came the two kidnappers. Mabon followed. They walked in silence. When they neared the meeting place, they stopped.

"We need to let the tribal council and the elders know what's happened. Can you make the short trip to their camp, Adam?" asked Nora. "But you shouldn't be alone. I can go with you."

"I'll go with him and we'll come right back," said Tish. "We'll be more careful this time, just in case."

Nora and Mabon looked from one to the other. Mabon shrugged. "Be careful," he warned. "Very careful."

Nora paused, and despite her concerns for their safety, took one last look into Mabon's eyes and said, "Okay, I guess. But please move slowly and carefully. And keep to the edges of the cleared paths. Come home by the inward trail. The one that's been laid out for emergencies. We'll take these chaps to our camp on the other side of the lake."

Chapter 11: Questions and Answers

Their arrival back in camp with two of the captured kidnappers caused a considerable stir among settlers and the wider community of forest people. Reactions varied; there were some of relief and pleasure, some of worry and concern at a set of circumstances that could put them all at risk. The captives were made as comfortable as possible while restrained in a well-guarded log storage building for the night, and an open meeting was set for late morning where everyone would have a chance to be present as many questions were posed to the culprits who had stolen away two of their well-loved young people. A few people were too restless and angry to sleep, but most of the people, local and visiting, returned to their various shelters and managed a decent night's rest.

In the morning, Mack and Elroy were fed a hearty breakfast of seeds and grains and fresh and dried fruit with milk from local goats. Afterwards they were taken to a sheltered wood beside the lake, given goat milk soap and towels, and told to clean and tidy themselves up. Both were loaned necessary clean clothing, stockings, and footwear. Mack wanted to wear his khaki uniform, but he was assured that the outfit was not appropriate and might make things even more difficult for him. A short time later both captives looked much less objectionable. Even Elroy looked acceptably decent. He certainly was cleaner and much more pleasant to be around. Mack grudgingly approved of the large and comfortable clothing he'd been given. Everything felt a bit snug on him, and some of the top shirt buttons had to remain undone, but he now looked quite presentable and far less threatening.

The meeting was to be held on the riverbank, and word had gone out overnight to several of the small settlements within a reasonable distance of the lake. Many forest people of various origins and backgrounds began to trickle in during the night, and the numbers increased as meeting time approached.

The sun was high when Nora stood to hush the chatter of the gathering crowd and begin the meeting. She asked the crowd for silence as the opening formalities of the meeting began; there would be ample time later for questions.

"We will begin by introducing our invited guests, and then we will ask Adam and Tish, who were abducted by the two of them, and Blanchfleur, who tracked and located them, and then Mabon and Nora, who captured them, and the others who helped, to join us up front. We will ask the accused the questions we need answered, and listen to their answers in silence. It is important to hear every word they speak. Is everyone happy with this approach?"

Nora paused a few minutes and the crowd heard only songbirds and insects and the gentle soothing lap of water against the lakeshore. Finally satisfied, she spoke. "We will begin then. Tish and Adam first."

Adam glanced at Tish and nodded. She seemed pleased but uncertain of herself. She pointed to herself and prepared to begin, while Adam nodded and smiled. She looked out over the large crowd of faces familiar and strange. She cleared her throat.

"Why?" she said clearly, then a pause and again asked, "Why?" She focused her attention directly on the faces of the two men perched on the stumps of two large birch trees that had been felled, cut in rounds, and split last winter for their fragrant firewood.

Elroy looked confusedly at Mack and blurted, "Moses."

"Moses," Tish repeated. "What is moses?"

"Moses is our boss," Elroy said. "He told us to go get some children and babies. He told us to find the people he heard were living up here and to get some kids and babies for our people."

There began an angry rumble of conversation among the large crowd. Nora raised her hand, palm toward the crowd, and the rumbling quickly ceased as the crowd pointed to the hand and shushed their mumbling neighbours. "Thank you," she said, and the chatter quieted. "Let the young ones ask their questions. And listen carefully and respectfully to the answers. We are here to learn from one another."

Adam stepped forward. He felt the anger of the crowd. He could read it in their faces, as menacing as the dark arrival of an approaching thunderhead, or the murderous voices of the Rangers bringing death and destruction into the Happy Valley years ago. He knew what they were feeling. "Was it you and your group, and your leader, Moses, who have been raiding the camps of the forest people and burning villages and injuring our friends and neighbours to the south?"

"I don't know nothing about that," said Elroy. He turned in near panic to Mack, who had been sitting and showing much agitation. Adam sensed that they were now truly feeling the people's anger and pain.

"We hurt no one," said Mack. "We didn't mean to hurt anyone. We don't burn and we don't kill."

"Then why would you take our babies and our children from us? Why did you kidnap Tish and me? What were you planning to do with us?'

"I don't know," said Elroy. "Moses said that the insiders of Aahimsa stole our lives from us. We got no families. We can't have no kids of our own. We should have had families. That's what Moses said."

The crowd began to murmur again. Nora and Mabon rose together and signalled for silence, which came instantly this time.

"But what about the families you took the children from? Don't they have the right to have families?" said Tish. "What about them? And what about the babies and the children? Don't they have a right to be with their own families?"

Elroy looked upset. "Yes, but what about us?"

Mack sat in silence through all this. He finally spoke. "I'm happy that you caught us. There may still be problems with Moses and the other guys. I don't know what's going to happen after they get here. But I hope you can find a better way. There must be a better way than hurting you."

Nora spoke. "You are relieved?" she said, her

voice angry. "How can you say that?" She was so confused by what Mack was telling them.

"Yes, I tried to stop Moses from sending us out on this wild scheme. I knew it wasn't smart or decent, but I seemed to be alone in my thinking," Mack said.

"If you weren't involved in the burning of villages and the violence, then who is?" asked Mabon.

"I don't know, but I've heard stories of a nasty bunch who were the last to get out of the Manuhome after the attack started and the big blast that wrecked everything. That bunch has workers from the most horrible workstation in the underground. They worked in the hell hole, servicing the red-hot ceramic pipes that brought up the city's energy from the hellish guts of the earth. All the others in the Manuhome and in the Agrihome looked down on those workers all their lives, called them the devil's demons. You were only sent to work there if you got into trouble up above, and once you got sent down there it was nearly impossible to return to work in the sunshine and the fields of the farms or the decent work conditions in most of the factories.

"I remember a guy they called Sparky who got sent down for setting a few fires in the Manuhome after he got drunk on some homemade liquor. He was always a bit unhinged, they said, a natural troublemaker who seemed able to attract a following of like-minded scoundrels. If it was him or his clowns who were the last out, they may hold the answer to your question." Mack paused a moment, looking hopefully at Nora, who had been listening carefully and beginning to have some understanding and sympathy. Then he sat down beside Leroy.

There followed a thoughtful silence and then Nora spoke. "How willing would you and your friend be to help us solve the problem you find yourselves in? What would happen if we decided to set you free?"

The listening crowd muttered and groaned a few moments, then sat as if stunned into silence. Nora turned to focus on them, and Mabon stepped forward beside her as if to protect her, his arms wide, his honest face drawing their attention to him. The crowd waited.

Mack coughed and cleared his voice, and then he spoke in a clear, respectful, almost unbelieving voice. "Could we stay here with you? Could we have a place to live?" He paused.

"Would you run away back to the others?" asked Mabon.

"I wouldn't," said Mack, and turned abruptly to face Elroy.

"What about you?" asked Nora, her eyes now pinning Leroy to the stump where he had been seated, listening to the words between his comrade and both Mabon and Nora.

"You mean it? We could maybe stay?" asked Elroy, his voice awkward and squeaky like an innocent child's. "And have a real home?"

"If you mean to stay and work hard and share with us like family members, then perhaps you could stay," said Nora.

Mabon spoke then. "We've never turned friends away. But if you prove to be our enemy, or you do something stupid like steal what is ours or what belongs to our neighbours again, we will take you somewhere you will never be found and leave you there." Mabon gave them his fiercest look.

"We'll work hard," said Elroy. "We learned how to work in the Manuhome. We know how to do a lot of things and we've never hurt anyone on purpose."

Nora turned back to the crowd. "It will be everyone's job to help our two new friends start a new life, and to keep an eye on them as well. We will soon know if we made a mistake. But we wish them well."

Tish stood up then and gestured to Adam, who quickly joined him. They spoke almost as one: "Let's all welcome them!"

The crowd rose then, at first tentatively and then in a rush, and together shouted "Welcome!"

before turning to the pair as if pleading with them to behave, before departing as slowly and as casually as they had arrived.

"Come with us," said Nora, and she and Mabon, Adam, and Tish led them to their temporary quarters while showing them around the village along the way. The two men followed, smiling, still astonished and hardly believing their good fortune.

Chapter 12:
Hen Returns
with Moses

It didn't take Moses long to realize that Henry had little memory of how far he had travelled from Mack and Elroy to Moses and the main camp. After travelling for more than an hour, they had stopped finding any signs of human passage.

"You really don't know where you're going, do you?" the leader asked, clutching his Bible close to his chest.

Hen was completely frustrated and, though he hated to admit that Moses was right, the redhead nodded.

Moses grimaced and turned to head back the way they had come. After twenty minutes or so he stopped, examined the trail, and found signs of recent passage. He kept going another five minutes and found where their path intersected with a slightly older sign, probably left by Hen, and after checking the location of the sun began to walk in a new direction. "Follow me," he said. He was not a natural-born tracker, but he was bright enough and learned quickly to find signs of human passage. He followed those signs until he found yet another spot where the signs of another trail crossed theirs. "Take a look here, Hen. The trail goes two ways. Take your time and decide which probably leads back to Mack and Elroy."

Hen went from one to the other, scratched his head, and finally decided. "This way." He pointed off to his left.

"Are you sure?" said Moses.

Hen shrugged. "Pretty sure," he said.

Moses grimaced and started off in the direction that Hen preferred, and within an hour they found themselves approaching what Hen was certain was the place where they would find his friends and their captives. He began to run and left Moses behind to make his way through thickly tangled trees and foliage.

"Holy crap!" Moses heard from the clearing ahead that was slowly opening itself up to him. When he caught up, Hen was running about the clearing as if looking for something. Moses found him kneeling beside what must have been the former campsite of Henry, Leroy, and Mack.

Chapter 13:
The Trackers

It didn't take long to find hundreds of signs left by the kidnappers and those others in search of the missing children. Joe Sam and Andrew had left the forest people's village after being given instructions and directions from the elders, who recently returned to camp from the waiting place. They learned that two of the newcomer young people from the old, once-abandoned village beside the small goose-shaped lake south of them had been kidnapped by three wild-looking outsider men who were armed with a rifle.

They learned from those same elders that Blanchfleur, the last mayor of the dead city of Aahimsa, had set out alone to follow the kidnappers and had asked the elders to return to their villages for help. Another villager, who met them at the meeting place, told them that Mabon, the powerful former ranger, and Nora, his partner, had recently set out to find and render aid to Blanchfleur. That was all they needed to know.

They followed an abundance of signs that any five-year-old forest child could have followed and soon discovered the spot where a few people had spent a few hours. No one was nearby at this moment as the birds were singing and calling in happy contentment.

The experienced Indigenous trackers spread out and searched the entire area and found the remains of a recent oversized and wasteful fire and a few unravelled strands left behind from old rope near one of the trees along the edge of the clearing.

"Stupid people," said Joe Sam. "They could have destroyed the forest and every living creature from here to the sea."

Andrew nodded. His angry face told the tale that he had been thinking the same thing.

They were discussing whether to carry on beyond the abandoned camp or to wait and see if anyone returned, when they heard loud voices and the rustle of grasses and branches that silenced the birds and even the insects, which meant people who didn't belong in this forest were approaching.

They hid quickly and comfortably in lots of time to observe the arrival of the loud and unsuspecting intruders. They didn't have long to wait.

Moses plunked himself down under a tree with a sigh and opened his leather-bound book and appeared to be reading from it. Henry joined him close to the tree and sat silently for a moment, trying to figure out where his compatriots might have gone. The fire pit looked like it had been cold for some time. Where could they have gone? It didn't make sense. And where were the two youngsters they had kidnapped?

After what seemed a long time, Moses closed his book. "And where are they, Henry?" he said.

Henry shrugged. He had no idea.

"Well, you had better have a look around and see what you can find," said Moses. He was speaking quite softly, and Hen knew soft speaking wasn't good where Moses was concerned. It usually meant he was not happy.

"Okay," said Hen. He began to weave in and out of the surrounding forest, but he neither heard nor saw anything unusual. He also didn't see Andrew come up silently behind him and put one large arm around his neck and the other over his mouth. Joe Sam then appeared in front of him and signalled for him to be silent and threatened the much smaller man by running his large, first finger across his wrinkled throat. Joe Sam was a powerfully built and tall man with a face that could be fierce when necessary. Fierce wasn't hard for him now as he recognized Henry, as the other man, obviously his superior, had called him.

"Now, Henry, we're going to sit down over here and wait for your boss man to come looking for you. I expect you won't want to warn him, because if you do, we'll have to hurt the two of you. Be a good fellow and nobody will get hurt. We would just like to have a word with the two of you. Your other friends are with companions of ours, and after a short while you can visit with them and we'll all have something to eat and drink and a talk. Nod if you understand and will behave."

Hen, whose red face was on fire and whose eyes mirrored his terror, managed a quick nod. He walked between the two huge men, and when the mean one pointed to a soft mound among the nearby trees, he sat. And they waited. A hoard of small ants climbed over his feet and tickled him, but he said nothing.

After a short while they heard a shout. "Henry! Where are you?"

Henry's eyes rolled back and forth. What could he do? He was terrified. Andrew, who sat across from Hen, caught his attention and shook his head while mouthing, "No."

After another minute or so of silence, they heard the boss man getting up, groaning noisily and impatiently, as if his knee joints were hurting him. They waited while he entered the trees close to where Hen had entered. He had no idea where they lay in wait. A few moments later he passed close by them, a revolver pointed out ahead of him. As he passed where Joe Sam waited, a large hand reached out and pulled the gun from his hand and tossed it deep into the dense surrounding trees. Joe Sam stepped toward him and pointed back in the direction the man had come. The man hesitated only long enough to consider his chances against this angry giant of a man before he turned and walked slowly back toward where Andrew stood beside the terrified Henry.

"What's his name, Henry?" asked Andrew.

"Moses," answered Hen.

"Okay," said Joe Sam. "We're all going to take a long walk. Then we'll eat and have a talk. We will make you a deal. If you behave, it can be a pleasant experience. If not, no promises. You can talk quietly if you want, but no shouting or noise. There are bears and wild dogs and a few crazy men around here, so the less said the better. Right, Andy?"

"That's a fact, brother," said Andrew. And they walked along as if they were friends or family. Two of them were quite worried about where they were being taken.

Chapter 14: Gathering Loose Ends

Kate, the chief of the forest people, arrived early for the second council meeting in the company of several elders and some of the youth, including her sons, Paul and Lone Cloud. Paul would be participating in the reconciliation hearing along with his mother, and Lone Cloud would be joining Joe Sam and Andrew, who would be entertaining Mack and Elroy in an underground food cellar. They had agreed to stay there for a short while before being brought out to meet a few others, including the forest people from the nearby new First Nations village, a few kilometres from their former village, now Mabon and Nora's home base.

Paul told his mother he wouldn't wander far, that he just wanted to find his friend, Adam, and ask for details about the kidnapping.

As he approached his young friend, Adam, now sixteen, Paul noticed that the boy had grown several hands higher since his arrival in the forest three years before. He stopped and watched as a canoe holding Tish and Alice and Blanchfleur appeared out of the distance and gradually come ashore. He continued to watch them as they pulled their canoe up onto the gravelled beach. Tish handed the woven bag she was carrying over to her mother and ran to meet her friends.

"Good," said Paul, smiling. He hurried to join Paul and Tish, his friendly eyes sparkling under his dark brows. "I can ask both of you about it."

"About what?" asked Tish.

"The kidnappers," said Adam. "There's not a lot to tell."

"Were you scared?" asked Paul. "I hear they had a gun."

"I'm pretty sure it wasn't loaded," said Adam.

"You didn't know that for sure!" said Tish. "He was scared, and so was I. But we didn't show it."

"Did they hurt you?" said Paul.

"They were rough, and they hit me on the head with their gun. But they didn't try to hurt us anymore once they had us with them. They only wanted to take us somewhere with them," said Adam.

"Why?" asked Paul.

"Their leader, Moses, is trying to gather up

babies and young people so he and his escaped Manuhome workers can have families," said Tish. "They couldn't have families."

"How do you know that?" asked Adam. "I didn't hear them say that."

"You were on the other side of the tree and maybe asleep. I was awake and heard them talking."

"Oh. Okay. If they could learn to live with us, they could share our families with us, couldn't they?…Unless they were the ones who were burning and hurting people." Paul was silent for a moment. "Because if they are…"

"Because if they are, what?" asked Tish.

"I don't think they are." said Adam.

"I don't know," said Paul. "We don't want to be threatened again, and we don't want to leave this place. We won't run ever again. I don't know what we would do."

Chapter 15: Second Riverbank Council

Adam, Tish, and Paul watched as Hen with his red, spiked hair and the man with the black book were led to their assigned places below the riverbank.

"Which ones are these?" asked Paul.

"The skinny one with the red hair was one of the kidnappers. The other one is probably his boss," said Adam.

"The one with the book doesn't look too scary. The other guy mostly looks confused," said Paul.

"Confused can be scary," said Tish to Paul. "Where is Lone Cloud? He's not with you?" Lone Cloud was her favourite of the forest people. He always teased her in his good-natured way, treating her like a little sister. And she had never had an older sibling. Adam teased her, too; he said Lone Cloud was her boyfriend. She always got a little mad when he said this and said not to be ridiculous, that Lone Cloud was too old and she still didn't like outsiders that much, even nice ones like Lone Cloud. Then he always said, "But you like me, don't you?" That always made her blush. She was thinking of this when Paul answered.

"Lone Cloud, Andrew, and Joe Sam are with the first of the kidnappers in the cold cellar along with the vegetables and the meat. They won't come out until the council gets to hear from these new visitors Andrew and Joe Sam brought back from the clearing where you and Adam were kept tied to that big tree."

"How did you hear that?" asked Adam.

"The whole forest has heard about what happened," said Paul. "There will be a big crowd from our village. Most of the elders want to be there to hear what these two know about the fires and the killings in the camps to the south."

Paul was right. As they spoke and watched, dozens of small groups, young and old, entered the area designated for the truth session on the riverbank.

Mabon and Nora were joined by Paul's mother, Kate, the chief of the Indigenous forest people, along with the many guests, a large crowd of elders, and the older newcomers. The youth who were around Adam and Tish's age gathered close to others their age and talked excitedly with Paul. Like young people everywhere, they had more in common with others their age than with their tribal elders. They had little interest in what mattered to the elders and they stayed mostly in the background, where many ran around and played kid's games and were by times too noisy, Tish thought. Though even they waited nervously for this meeting to start.

Nora and Kate got to their feet and the latter motioned for silence. The excited chatter gradually stopped, and even the smallest of the children ceased their play and moved to the outside fringes of the crowd, seeking out parents and relatives. Nora nodded to the chief who then confidently approached Hen and Moses.

All attention was on Kate as she paused, and the crowd became ever more silent. Even the smallest of birds could be heard singing in the distant trees, and the smallest breaking wave seemed magnified.

"I welcome all who have come to have questions answered by these latest visitors to our former camp, home for us for many happy years and now the peaceful home to the many recent additions to our forest people. We welcomed all who came here in peace as they fled the destruction of the walled cities and the insiders who threatened their lives and their safety. The last three years have been prosperous and richly satisfying to all of us who have chosen to live together as one large, cooperating family. It is in this same spirit of hope and confidence in the goodness that lies within all people that so many of us have gathered here to speak to these latest strangers who have been disturbing the peace of our home places and our minds."

She turned her eyes on Hen and Moses. "We have gathered today to hear your stories. We want to understand why you would come in the night and steal the babies and children of our people and the children of our neighbours. To leave our people puzzled, alone, and frightened: the children, their parents, and whole communities who know and love them. We have all heard what the first two kidnappers said. We heard and understood about not having children of your own and not having families. But there are many among us who have no children. None of us own our children. They are young people of the forest and are the children of all our people. That is why all of our people are upset with you and the others."

She paused a moment to let what she had said sink in. Then she turned her attention once more to the seated kidnappers. Henry, with his spiked and greased red hair, and the tall, golden-haired Moses, with his black Bible clutched tightly in his hands, his neat trousers and spotless white shirt, and the long white scarf that he wore around his neck hanging down on both sides in front of him like a clergyman's stole.

Kate pointed to Henry and signalled for him to stand up. Henry rose, looking frightened, as the crowd's eyes bored into him like hot irons, many barely able to contain their anger and disdain. "You are Henry," she said, "sometimes called Hen."

Henry scowled. He hated to be called Hen. "How do you know what others call me?" he snapped.

"We know more than that," the chief continued, always patient. "You are the one who crept into our village and tried to steal one of our babies. You ran away and dropped him on the ground like a lump of spoiled meat."

Henry lowered his eyes in shame and appeared to be on the verge of tears when Kate spoke again.

"Fortunately for you, the child was sturdy and not injured. But there was harm done to his parents and to all of us. Our peaceful world became temporarily a world of fear and uncertainty." She gestured for Hen to sit down and Moses to stand.

"I wasn't around here when this happened," Moses said. "I didn't get here until yesterday."

The crowd groaned and began to shout "Boss, boss." They began a chant and rose to their feet. It appeared that they might rush the two visitors at any moment.

The chief raised her hand and the crowd silenced and sat.

"They know who you are, too. They said you are their boss. The other visitors who arrived in camp just before you told us about you and why they were sent to steal our children and bring terror to our villages. What we want to know now is if you set fire to the villages not far from here and injured peaceful people of the forest. What do you know of this?"

"We didn't burn or injure," yelled Henry. "We didn't want to hurt no one."

Kate turned toward Moses, who was clutching his leather-bound book and worrying his dangling scarf with nervous fingers. He was shaking his head slowly back and forth. "No, we didn't mean any harm to villages or people," he said.

"Do you know of any others like you who might do harm, who might burn or kill?" Nora asked.

"I don't," said Moses. "I'm so sorry about all of this."

"I heard something about some of the oilers from the pit," said Henry. "The greasers I worked with were talking a couple of times about someone named Sparky who liked to burn things. That's why he got sent to work in the deepest part of the pit, where the ceramic pipes go down. It is terribly hot and sweaty down there all the time, and everyone is grumpy and full of hate for everyone up above. Sparky might have escaped during the attack on the homeland with a bunch of friends from down there. There was a guy called Earl, a Watts, a Gin, and a guy called Pipes. I heard their names, but that's all I heard. Some of them might do something like that."

The two men were led away to meet in private with Kate and the elders and to be reunited with Mack and Elroy. After that it would be decided if they would be offered a chance to join the people or be exiled or punished in some other way.

Chapter 16:
The Plan Develops

Mack and Elroy had sat silently but restlessly under the supervision of Lone Cloud, Joe Sam, and Andrew. There hadn't been much talk at first between the five men. Lone Cloud had heard a few of the rumours about what had happened and was filled with curiosity.

"Are there just the four of you? Or are there more of you out there? And are you all a bunch of kidnappers, looters, and starters of fires?" he asked.

Mack looked at Elroy, but the larger man slouched and stared at his large feet that were sporting a pair of oversized moccasins he had been handed to replace the filthy boots he had arrived in. His borrowed shirt was hanging completely open as its few carved buttons were no match for his still massive, distended belly. Mack had somehow come out of the clothing change arrangements looking much more presentable and, due to the kindness of his captors, he was feeling more relaxed and comfortable in the clean, simple clothing he had been loaned.

"I explained all this at the meeting," Mack said.

"I wasn't present at the meeting...Answer me, please. I'd like to hear it from you," Lone Cloud persisted.

"Who are you, anyway?" asked Mack.

"I am called Lone Cloud," he said. "My mother is the chief of our village."

"I see," said Mack. "Well, Lone Cloud, my man Elroy and myself explained that we were sent out by our chief, who calls himself Moses, to gather up some people, mostly young people, so we could have families and start a town of our own."

"And why can't you have families of your own?" asked Lone Cloud.

"We were sterilized when we were children and sent to work in the Manuhome or the Agrihome. Now we are free to do as we wish, but we can never live like normal people; we can never have children or families. We only wanted what has been taken away from us by the insiders and the City of Aahimsa."

"But we are not the people of Aahimsa. We have taken nothing from you. Why would you steal our families?"

There was a long pause and Mack sat wringing his hands, his eyes on the bare patch of ground before him. Finally, he lifted his face and looked Lone Cloud in the eye. His voice was shaking. "I guess we weren't thinking of you, only ourselves."

"And the fires and the injuries?" continued Lone Cloud, "What about those?"

"That wasn't us. Those were bad people. Maybe Sparky's people," said Elroy. "We just never thought. Do you think we could ever be part of your people?"

"Probably not. You could never live in peace with us. We are a peaceful people. We do not want trouble and crime inside our villages."

"Maybe we could learn to live in peace," said Mack. "If you give us a chance. We could learn."

Lone Cloud looked over at Joe Sam and Andrew. "What do you think?" he asked.

Joe Sam and Andrew looked at one another and each shrugged. "Maybe," said Joe Sam. "Maybe."

Paul, Adam, and Tish came to the root cellar and led the five to one of the larger village teepees. The eight of them joined Paul and Lone Cloud's mother, Kate, the chief, and five elders from council of the forest people along with Nora and Mabon and Alice and Blanchfleur, and the two latest guests, Moses and Henry.

The chief asked everyone to sit in a circle around a small fire in the centre of the comfortable enclosure perfumed with the not unpleasant scent of hundreds of previous fires and wisps of smoke from the present one that smelled sweetly of white birch and the percussive snapping needles of fresh spruce and fir twigs.

"We will sit a while as a family would and decide if it might be possible to continue to remain as such a family. The elders and I have been thinking that we just might have an answer to the question we have been discussing lately at several of our council meetings. How are we to deal with the burnings and the murders and the stealing of children without destroying the peace and prosperity that we have seen building and growing strong in our forest over the past few years? It is our wish that we may live in peace and share what we have with our good neighbours. We do not want to fight with anyone, but we cannot sit by and watch our homes be destroyed and our people harmed.

"So, my next question is: Can we, with our different histories and backgrounds, live together and work together to peacefully put an end to dangers that are threatening our forest and our people?

And my final question is: Are all of us here and the people we represent willing to work together and try?"

Nora, Mabon, Blanchfleur, Alice, Tish and Adam spoke as one. "We are willing. We can do it."

Moses looked at his handful of followers and nodded. The others nodded too. "We're in," he said, "if you'll give us a chance."

Lone Cloud stood up and faced Moses and his henchmen. "What about the other people like you that you have in hiding not far from here?"

Moses also stood. "I will invite them, and many of them will want to join us. This is better than the stupid, thoughtless plan we had. If you will accept us as part of your family, we will come here and with your help, we will learn to live and work with you."

Blanchfleur rose up then, with Alice at her side. Tish and Adam also rose up to get a better view, as Blanchfleur, the once powerful mayor of Aahimsa, the grandmother of Tish, spoke: "But are you truly capable of living in peace? Can you help us stop this Sparky person and his villains without resorting to violence? I willingly accept the blame and the guilt for my hand in your inability to have families. I hope that you will someday understand the irony that I also saved your lives by the same actions that ruined them.

"We can talk about this later. But now we must have peace. It is our only hope if we are to continue to exist as people. Are you willing and able to put aside all differences and to join us as neighbours and friends and to share in the blessings of all the families, adults and children, who live here in the forest?"

"Yes, I'm sure we can do it. If we can be part of your family, we can do anything you ask of us."

"But can we find a way to do it without starting a war, even a small one?" asked Nora.

"I think we can," said Moses. "But it won't be easy."

The chief and the elders had been standing by silently until then. She raised her hand and she spoke. "Enough for now," she said. "In the morning I will pick a small group from all parties to travel with Moses to find his people and lead those who opt for a new life with us back here. We will meet with them, and if they agree to join with all of us to formulate a plan, then we will do it.

"Then we will go into the wild places and we will root out Sparky and the other evil ones and we will capture them and find a way to either fix them or exile them to places they will never return from. Agreed?" she said.

There was a roar of agreement, and then all set out to enjoy an evening's rest.

Chapter 17: Sparky and the Gang

Sparky and the gang were hurting. Their activities had netted them all the food they could carry and more bows and arrows and hunting spears than they could hope to ever use. The last raid was days past and fresh, edible food was quickly getting scarce.

They had done some terrible things to the villages they had ransacked and burned. They had seriously injured at least a few of the villagers. But they themselves hadn't gone unscathed. They had lost several of their number through injury and a couple who had been injured and later died after both the old and experienced, and the young and fit among the villagers, fought frantically, shoulder to shoulder, to protect their families or children.

Several of the more ferocious survivors of the skirmish, original members of Sparky's group, had deserted their violent companions after discovering how viciously and inhumanely they were being expected to behave. Their numbers had now been whittled down to five, and all five were not happy to remain a part of the group.

Sparky and Gin were the core and the instigators of the worst behaviour. Earl, Watts, and Pipes were close to setting off on their own, but hesitated for a variety of reasons. The greatest fear was the obvious lack of human decency and the near madness and unpredictability of the two would-be leaders. In addition, there was the reality that all three of the discontented companions had no idea where in the world they were, or how close to being apprehended by the many enemies they had made, or if they even knew enough to survive on their own. Both Sparky and Gin had worked above ground at the Manuhome for years, before being sent underground, and should know something about how to grow food and how to find it. They might even know ways to prepare and cook it.

All sat in silence around the small fire in the dry cave that Watts had discovered a few hours ago as he walked along the sand on the rugged coast. The miserable group had actually taken time to thank him for finding and providing such a safe and comfortable hideaway.

They were all cold, exposed to the damp evening air off the crashing sea beside them. They had been walking for what seemed hours and the night with its snakes and coyotes and wild dogs and hooting owls and its hungry bears was closing in. The tide had lowered, and Watts had been able to see the gaping mouth of the opening in the stone cliff and was disappointed that open water kept him from exploring, as a tidal stream had eroded a deep trench that ran from the ocean to the inside of the cave.

There remained, however, a few minutes before complete sunset, so he opted to climb a path he had spotted a few dozen yards back that he thought might lead to the cliff top and another way inside the rocky cave. He followed the sandy pathway and found that a natural trail led from the bank above down to a large shelf inside a large dry cave, several feet above the tidal ocean stream and the natural pool that lay within.

Once settled on the inside with their gear and supplies, Gin had built a fire and cooked and they had eaten well from the deer that Sparky had shot that afternoon to supplement the vegetables, grains, and pulses they had stolen on their last raid. Despite the tasty and hearty meal that Gin had prepared, Sparky was in a terrible temper and Gin glared at the three others.

"Sparky says to hand over the guns and bullets we gave you," Gin said. "I don't remember seeing any of you actually using them, anyways."

Watts was the first to rise and fetch his rifle and dig a handful of cartridges from his sand-filled jacket pocket. "There" he said.

Gin took the long gun and handed it and the ammo to Sparky, who opened his hand and looked at the bullets. "There are only six," he said. "We gave twelve to each of you."

Watts shrugged. "That's all I got," he said. "I fired a couple at the raids. I guess the rest fell out of my pocket."

Sparky raised the carbine in his hands and made as if to hit Watts with the stock, and Watts fell to the floor of the cave. His hands protected his head and his scream echoed around the cave. Gin laughed and stepped to where the other two sat. "Hand them over," he said.

"You can have the gun," said Pipes. "I fired two bullets at a goose one day and missed. I fired a few at one of the raids and Gin asked me to give him some bullets. I don't have any more."

"Is he lying?" asked Sparky. His face almost demonic in the firelight. Sparky didn't like to wash his face or his hands. He said it was for camouflage, but it stayed the same even when there was lots of time between raids and travels.

"I may have got a couple of bullets from him. I swear I never even saw him try to aim at anybody. But I sure as hell didn't take all of them." Pipes waited for someone to attack him. He had thrown his other bullets away, one at a time—intentionally. He had no interest in hurting anyone. When nothing happened, he sat on the damp stone floor.

"How about you, Earl?" asked Sparky. "Did you lose yours, too?"

"I must have fired them all," he said.

"How many of those villagers did you hit?" asked Gin.

"I don't know," said Earl. He shrugged. "I never fired a gun before."

"I see," said Sparky. "How many bullets you got left, Gin?"

"With the six he gave me," he said, pointing at Watts, "I've ten. How about you?"

"Eight or ten," said Sparky. "We'll have to go looking for more. There are lots of old abandoned buildings north of here. We'll need bullets before we do another raid."

"But we don't need these three bums. They don't want to be part of this," yelled Gin, and he grabbed Pipes by the arm and yanked him to his feet.

"Ouch, go easy, Gin. My arm still hurts where I got burned on those steam pipes," Pipes yelled in his high-pitched voice.

"Aw, your burns. Too bad. I'll cool your burns," he said, and Gin shoved Pipes off the stone shelf, down into the pitching waves that had begun to pound the inner cave walls as the tide rose and the stormy ocean outside rushed in, slammed the wall of the granite cave, then rolled over and ran angrily, frothing its way out of the cave to be swallowed into the dark green ocean outside.

Pipes disappeared under the swirling water and rose again near the mouth of the cave long enough to scream, "I can't swim," before disappearing down under again and being slammed against the water-drenched back wall of the large stone cave.

Sparky had then grabbed Watts and tossed him into the salty brine alongside Pipes, and in that moment, Earl had risen, and full of rage, tossed Gin into the now boiling soup of churning sea water. Earl saved himself as he jumped from the rock shelf into the water and was able to get a firm grip on the back of his friend Pipes's shirt, and he began to swim strongly with the now outflowing current. He saw that Watts was also swimming strongly outwards as Gin managed to scramble up on the wet rocks and onto the stone ledge on the opposite side of the pool across from Sparky.

Outside the cave, where the moon had shaken off the clouds and was bouncing chunks of light off the rolling breakers of the green Atlantic, Earl dragged Pipes up on the first bar of sand they came to and they found that Watts was already waiting there, shivering in the ocean breeze, anxious to lend a hand. "Let's get going," he said. "I know the way from here. Let's put some beach between us and them."

"Will they follow us?" asked Pipes.

"I doubt it. Not now. Sparky can't swim, and he and Gin are on opposite sides of the pool. When the tide drops and the water settles, Gin will swim out and meet Sparky at the path on top. But I figure they're glad to be rid of us. I doubt if any of us have any interest in helping those two find more bullets," said Earl. "There's a good moon; let's get as far away from here as we can."

"What about our stuff?" asked Watts. "And our food?"

"We can get along. We have no choice, have we? There's food all around us, and these woods are full of old abandoned buildings, so we should be able to find stuff. We may even be able to find other people we'll be able to live with who aren't completely out of their rotten minds."

Chapter 18: Trouble in the Sea Cave

Gin stood in safety atop the wet shelf about ten metres away, separated from Sparky by a pool of thrashing water. He yelled to get Sparky's attention, finding it was all he could do to make himself heard above the splashing and banging of the huge waves as they slammed violently into the cave, battered the back wall, and then spun around and hurried back out. The brutal energy of the surging water seemed like it would never soften and ease up.

"I'm catching the next wave out that looks calm enough," he yelled.

He saw that Sparky was saying something in return as the arsonist was moving his mouth. But Gin had no idea what his partner in crime had said. "Stay there," he yelled, "and I'll follow them; try to see where they're going."

"Okay," Sparky shouted back. There had been a momentary lull between the crashing waves and Gin heard what his boss had said. He watched as Sparky stepped to the wall directly behind where he had, until then, been standing at the edge of the pool, and he plunked himself down against the wall. Gin gave a brief parting wave and dove into the pool. He enjoyed the sensation as a large return wave carried him toward the faint light entering the cave entrance.

Moments later he was wishing he had swum faster because a heavier wave came at him, pushing him back almost to the rock wall behind him. He took another deep breath and gathered himself to catch the next outward flow, and when he did, he swam as frantically as he was able. A few seconds later he found himself scraping his body aground against a bar of gritty sand and gravel beneath a bright moon and signs of a calming sea and brilliant starry sky.

He scurried up the sand and pebbles beside the stream and looked around, not knowing what to expect. It was possible that the others lurked somewhere about, and he was aware he was unarmed. He now knew that he would be no match for Earl in a hand-to-hand encounter and besides, he was outnumbered three to one.

He decided he was in no rush to catch up, so he would simply take his time. Sparky would wait. Sparky was his boss. He was smart enough, and tough enough as long as he had a gun and others didn't. But boss or no boss, it didn't matter much, because he knew Sparky was soft and a coward, even if he was as crazy as those spooky-sounding loons that frightened him with their eerie calls as he lay awake at night in the wild. Better to wait a while for the others to get as far away as possible and get himself some rest. Afterwards he could climb up the cliff face and enter the cave by land. Then he and Sparky could figure out how many bullets they had for their gun and go looking for more weapons and ammo. The more he thought about it, the more he realized they were better off by themselves; no point in dragging those useless cowards along to share in their loot and to cause them more trouble.

Chapter 19: The Seekers

Kate, the chief of the forest people village, asked Nora and Mabon to help organize a combined group to scout out the territory around their two communities, branching out and extending as far as was practical. She had been talking with her elders, who had been in contact with inhabitants of both groups concerned about dangerous strangers arriving on a much-too-regular basis. All agreed that, though it was their policy to welcome strangers, it was clear, even after the positive experience of welcoming the recent arrivals from Aahimsa, that there were strangers out there who might pose dangers to all of them. The proposed group, which she said would be named The Seekers, would be on the lookout for any unfamiliar outsiders who might be lurking within easy reach of their villages.

There had been no rumours of recent attacks by the fire-setting murderers who had burned distant villages to the ground, but the existence of such a group had been confirmed by tribal visitors at the recent council meetings. She suggested a mixture of young and old from the forest people and from Mabon and Nora's group who had come to be trusted neighbours, including Blanchfleur and even perhaps a representative from the recently arrived kidnappers who might be able to identify one or more of the arsonist murders.

Blanchfleur suggested the group be headed up by Mabon, Nora, and Joe Sam and include Adam and Tish and her two boys, Paul and Lone Cloud. She would ask for a couple of volunteers from her council, and Mabon and Nora could add whom they wished.

"What about that new lot? Who would you suggest?" asked Nora.

"How about the one they call Mack? He seems reasonably sane," said the chief. "And maybe the big guy, Elroy."

"I'm not too sure about that one," said Mabon, as he worried the tips of his long brown hair now fringed with white, his blue eyes grown lighter and more mystical with the passing years. "He's not easy to handle."

"He might come in handy if we needed him," said Nora. "I think this might give us a chance to find out how sincere these two are about joining us on our terms. We would have to keep an eye on them, of course," she added. "None of them have had much a chance to act in any way but tough and hard."

"When should we start?" asked Mabon after a long silence where he pondered Nora's words. She was probably right as usual. At least, he hoped she was.

"I'll send our group over tomorrow morning. We should get started right away," said the chief. "I may come along with you myself…We'll see." She smiled, showing her strong white teeth, her dark brown eyes gleaming in her kind face.

It was decided that the young people and the elders should work together and travel a wide swath in a circle that spiralled the two villages. Anyone who came upon persons or groups would signal the others around them, and they would come together and decide how best to deal with the intruders.

"There will be no heroes, there will be no violence except to prevent a tragedy," said Nora. "No one will be completely in charge, but for now,

Mabon and Blanchfleur and the chief and her elders asked me to be the one who makes final decisions. Do you all agree?"

There were murmurs of agreement and nods, all around.

"Alice and Blanchfleur and Kate will look after things at home while we are away from our camps."

"The young people will travel in a group with me," Nora said, stepping up on a small grassy mound amidst the growing throng. "All except Paul, who will stay close to Mabon and Mack and Elroy. The elders from the forest people's camp will divide themselves equally among our two groups. We will travel in near silence and keep our ears and eyes tuned to the natural sounds of the forest. If there are intruders who do not belong here, the living forest will let us know.

"My group will form a circle moving to the left and Mabon's group will circle to the right. When we next cross paths, we will exchange information, then expand the circle outward and continue onward, covering a wider area. Should any of you discover strangers or any signs of unknown intruders, give four owl hoots, and wait a slow count of ten. Then give three more hoots and count again to ten, then two hoots and count. Anyone who hears your repeated pattern of calls will move quietly toward the sound and wait for others to arrive. As for the trackers, Paul or Lone Cloud, or Joe Sam, or perhaps Mabon. Remember we want to find these people and bring them safely to a meeting; we do not want to scare them off or harm them. Do you understand?" The tracker group responded with nods and much patting of shoulders.

"Remember, no haste and move quietly," said Mabon. "Try and travel without telling the entire forest that we are here. Let's begin," he said, and he set off to the right, all his followers moving close behind in near silence.

"Are the rest of you ready?" Nora said to Adam and Tish, Lone Cloud and Joe Sam, and a handful of elders. They picked up their packs and headed in their expanding circle to the left. Adam walked to the right of Tish with Lone Cloud on her left. The forest smelled of fresh evergreen buds and newly awakening ferns. Nora breathed in the welcome perfume of the healthy forest, looked back at her followers, and warmly smiled.

Chapter 20: Watts, Pipes, and Earl Abroad

Watts, Earl, and Pipes had quickly left the ocean behind and climbed the path up the cliff, carefully turning away from the sea cave at the top and hurrying along the path that led to an old abandoned highway that once was covered in thick pavement and was now broken and overgrown with grasses and small trees. They came to another abandoned bit of roadway, reduced to a few chunks of broken pavement. They had travelled from the south and so decided to continue farther north, aware of the possibility of colder winters, in order to get as far away from their dangerous former companions as they possibly could.

The evening was nearly gone, and complete darkness was descending on them as heavy dark clouds walled them off from the moon and the stars. It now occurred to Earl that they were completely on their own in the coal-black wilderness.

"Let's light a fire," he said.

"Not a great idea," said Watts.

"How come?" asked Earl.

"Let me guess," said Pipes. "We don't want those two apes to find us. That's one."

"I think it's going to pour rain," he said. "And besides. I got no matches. How about you?"

"Anyone got anything to eat?" asked Watts.

"Nope," said Earl.

"Nope," said Pipes.

"What are we going to eat?" asked Earl.

"Nothing," said Pipes.

"What are we going to do?" asked Earl.

"I saw the ruins of an old building far up ahead before the light left us. If we hurry, we can get there before the rain starts."

"The rain?" said Earl.

"What do you think those black clouds meant?" said Pipes. "We'll get some shelter and we'll try to dry off and get a bit of sleep. We'll find something to eat tomorrow."

"Where are we headed for?" asked Earl.

"Your guess is as good as mine," said Watts. "We're going to put some space between Sparky and Gin and their pockets full of bullets. We're going to try and find someplace we can live without guns and bullets, and we're going to find some way to feed ourselves and build a fire and a few other things. But let's get to that building Pipes saw as soon as we can. One step at a time."

Chapter 21: Seeking

By the fourth day, Adam and Tish and Lone Cloud had moved well ahead of the rest of their group, and with their youth and stamina had been pulling the others in their group a bit faster than Nora and Joe Sam thought wise. Tish was the first to hear the series of hoots behind them.

"Hold on," she said, slowing. She tugged at Adam's shirt, and when Adam stopped, Lone Cloud noticed. He turned and waited. "Listen," Tish said.

"Come on," said Adam once he and Lone Cloud heard the hoots back in the near distance behind them. They all were running now, passing a few of the others who lagged behind them.

They quickly arrived back where Nora and Joe Sam and the two elders waited. The group was sitting quietly under the shade of a massive oak tree.

"What's up?" asked Adam. "Have you found someone?"

"No," said Nora. "You three adventurers have been setting too fast a pace. You run the risk of catching your prey and yourselves by surprise."

"You are going much too fast for the rest of us to be of any help to you," said Joe Sam. "At the rate you're taking us, we are likely to step into trouble we can't handle. Remember, they have at least one gun. We don't want to catch up to gunfire and dead or wounded companions."

"Sorry," said Adam. Lone Cloud took up a position between him and Tish. He felt embarrassed but said nothing.

"We were hoping to be the first to find someone," said Tish.

"We understand," said Nora, "but we have to be sensible. We want to be able to surprise them, but not by stumbling into their midst. These may be the goons who have harmed and burned out our neighbours. This is no game. If you want to share the lead, or even be the leaders, you are going to have to use good judgement.

"Joe Sam, Lone Cloud, and the elders will lead, and the rest of us will follow quietly behind. If anyone hears anything suspicious, we'll signal and go to ground. We'll wait until we know where the sound came from. Joe Sam is the tracker. He will find them, and he and Lone Cloud will help us come up with a plan."

Joe Sam had listened patiently and, when he was satisfied that Nora had stopped speaking, he stepped forward and raised a hand, palm forward. He smiled and spoke softly. "The youngsters can come with us. It will be safe. We will not go near the fugitives until we have watched them make a camp and sleep. Then we should not have to fear their guns."

Nora hesitated briefly, then nodded agreement.

The youngsters, Joe Sam, Lone Cloud, and the forest people elders moved along at a careful, steady pace the following day, and near dusk Lone Cloud signalled quietly for a halt. He sniffed the forest air noisily and pointed off into the dense evergreens to his left. The others sniffed the fragrant air too. Amid the rich smells of ferns and evergreens and the sweet grasses, they all understood. Tish was the first to speak. "Smoke," she whispered. "Wood smoke."

Joe Sam gave the agreed-upon signals. Adam was impressed by the realistic hoots of the tracker and Lone Cloud and the elders, compared to less authentic calls he and Tish could produce. He had heard Mabon and Nora reproduce the calls okay, too, but never as real sounding as the forest people could do them.

Ten minutes later the group huddled together in a small clearing as they waited for Joe Sam to go ahead and investigate and return with his information.

More than a couple of hours went by, and the youngsters had begun to worry that something bad had happened to the tracker when he popped up almost soundlessly behind them as they stared into the direction he had taken when he set out. He stepped easily into their midst and squatted on his haunches. He was smiling and seemed perfectly relaxed.

He held up three fingers. "Three of them, hiding out in a withered wooden barn. All grown men. One of them was sobbing like a baby, saying over and over that he was hungry and he didn't want to die. The other two had found water to drink and tried to give some to their hungry friend. But he refused as if he preferred to moan and groan. They have a large fire going inside the barn. If they don't burn themselves to death, they will soon sleep, and we will disarm them and escort them back to camp. I didn't see a gun or any packs that could contain guns or food. If we offer them food and shelter, they will likely be happy to come peacefully along with us."

\\

By the time they left their temporary camp, the plans were made. They would enter the barn in the dark. Joe Sam would lead Lone Cloud and the elders to each of the sleeping fugitives in turn. He would cover each victim's mouth while the others held legs and arms until each was gagged and bound. When all three had been disabled, and not till then, they would speak to their captives and make the offer of help and assure them of their safety if they cooperated.

He led his crew in the pitch-black night across clearings and woods as if it were in daylight and confidently entered the barn, going first to Earl, as it seemed he might pose the greatest challenge. Joe Sam blew a faint whistling sound through his lips and the four men pounced together.

Earl awoke with a start and opened his eyes to complete darkness. Not even the faintest light entered through the open doorway or the shattered and dirt-stained windows of the old abandoned wooden barn. Even the last embers of the campfire had gone dark. He was terrified and, other than for a few feeble grunts, lay quiet and still while whatever had landed on him wrapped him up in strips of cloth and bits of rope. Then the aggressors left him lying there while he listened to the brief whimpers and useless struggles of his barn mates.

What seemed an endless night of silence followed, before the first glow of sunrise began to illuminate the darkness in the barn and he was able to make out the forms of his pals trussed up in a fashion very similar to the bindings holding him captive. Moments later, several imposing figures rose up from around them and stood circling them.

"We're going to take off your gags and you can yell all you want, but nobody but us will hear you. So, I hope that instead of yelling, you will listen carefully," said Nora. "We're here to offer you our help. I expect you are hungry and tired. You might even be scared. But I assure you that you are in no immediate danger from us."

Adam and Tish and Lone Cloud carefully removed the cloth gags and the three men waited in silence. Earl was the first to speak.

"I'm starving. We haven't eaten anything decent for days. Do you have any food?"

"We'll share what we have, and if you agree, we'll take you somewhere safe where there is plenty to eat and you can talk to our assembly. Perhaps we can find a way to live in peace and find ways to help one another."

Joe Sam and the elders then released the captives from their ropes and bindings. The three men rose and stretched while what food their captors had at hand was shared among all present, and they together, like old friends, set out for the forest people's camps as rapidly as the weary and weakened threesome could manage.

After an hour's march they met up with Mabon's band of seekers coming from the other direction. They paused long enough to share skins of fresh drinking water and fill Mabon's group in on the tactics and successes of their operation.

Mabon approached the three newcomers and looked them in the eye. They gazed at the huge former Ranger and sensed the power of his presence. Mabon had a way of sympathetically seeing into and understanding people he met. He sensed hope mixed with the fear in the captives' response to him.

He understood that these three men were used to hard treatment over their entire lives. He had met others like them during his training as a Ranger in his youth. Ueland could be harsh in his treatment of troublesome workers, and these three had the demeanour of mistreated puppies.

"Do any of you know who was attacking villages to the south?" he asked.

The three glanced nervously toward one another.

"Yes," said one of them with a surprisingly squeaky voice.

"What's your name?" asked Mabon.

One of the others laughed. Mabon glanced toward that one and the grin immediately left his plump face as he said, "I never knew his real name, but everyone calls him Pipes. He was a plumber at the Manuhome."

"And the rest of you? Your names?" said Mabon.

"I'm Earl," said the larger, tall man who had remained silent through all this.

"They call me Watts," said the shorter, broader man who had named Pipes. He rocked from side to side when he moved, like a sailor, and he was rocking now as he waited for Mabon's further questions.

"Okay. I think you had something to do with the brutality and the burning of the villages of the southern forest people, our neighbours and friends."

"It wasn't us. We never really hurt anyone," said Pipes. "We were there, but we hated what they were doing, and we ran away from the two killers."

"Gin and Sparky," said Earl. "Two real nasty guys. They even tried to kill us, and so we ran away. They're probably coming after us now."

"You head back to camp with the others and we'll talk soon. Joe Sam will come with me and perhaps one of the elders."

"I want to go with you," said Adam.

"Me, too," said Tish.

"No, I want you to stay with Nora and help out

in getting everyone and everything settled back in camp. We'll hold a council when we get back. In the meantime, do all you can to help. I'll see you soon."

Chapter 22:
Sparky and
Gin Stay Put

Gin discovered the rough steps that would lead up to the right of the tidal stream that flowed in and out of the cave. They steeply scaled the cliff face, and after a few short steps along the bank he turned sharply downward by a narrow path to an alternate entrance into the sea cave, or the abandoned mine, or, whatever it was. Instead of going directly back to deal with Sparky, he decided to take shelter from the cool sea breeze and try to snatch some much-needed rest. He would leave Sparky all by himself in the damp, dark cave long enough to stew in his lonely, self-inflicted predicament so he could have a chance to settle down.

Gin figured he knew the boss better than anybody. By morning Sparky would be ready to scream with frustration and loneliness, and that was great because he wanted his nutty boss to appreciate the fact that his best pal, Gin, had returned, and he was no longer alone in the wilderness. Either that or he might be ready to shoot his only friend in the world. But no, their bullets were too scarce to waste on murdering his only friend and ally.

Gin chuckled to himself as he burrowed beneath the thick, low-lying branches of a tall, wide-skirted spruce and lay down on the mound of soft, spicy needles underneath. The evening felt warm there, out of the wind, and in minutes he felt himself drifting into sleep.

He was awakened by the rustling of undergrowth and the emergence of a small black-and-white animal with a long, furry tail, closely followed by three smaller versions of herself. As he noted the white stripe that began behind her head and split into two separate paths up along her back to her bushy tail, he simultaneously sensed an acrid, eye-watering reek and realized what she was. He had never seen a skunk up close, but he had heard lots about them. He scrambled to his feet to get out from under the tree, but the heavy, needle-laden branches sent him hard down on the ground as the terrified lady went into action to protect her children.

Gin's rough face was close enough to the animal to experience not only the suffocating effects of the spray but also the burning, blinding pain the acidic, sticky substance inflicted on his eyes. He cried out in desperation and curled into a tight ball and wept and desperately wiped his face with his needle-covered hands and then his dirty shirttail, until his scalding eyeballs cleared enough to allow his eyesight to slowly return.

An hour ago, he had been certain that he would die from the stench, but, despite the intensity of it, he realized that he could never escape the stink by dying. Eventually, though, he decided that the smell had mostly gone away (as his now-numb nose could no longer smell it) and he set off to rescue his lonesome partner from his misery alone in the sea cave.

His journey to the entrance of the cave took only minutes, and he was almost able to enjoy the gradual rising of the sun and the morning's growing warmth, and the blessed freshness that blew onshore from the ocean. He wondered if Sparky was going to be excited when he arrived at the cave.

He could now see enough to pick out the bit of rusted railing that marked the steps that led down into the cave, and he hurried down the steps and burst into the cave with a yell that woke the sleeping Sparky, who stumbled to his feet and took up his gun.

"Out!" he yelled. "Get outside, or I'll shoot you. You stink. How did you manage to get yourself sprayed by a skunk? You idiot! Get out!"

"We need to talk," said Gin.

"Not in here, not now, we don't. Go back out and climb back up to the top of the bank. I'll wait a few minutes and talk to you from down here, outside. Your stupid face is still caked with spruce needles and that disgusting polecat spray."

"I'll go back down to the sea and wash it off," said Gin.

"Go then," said Sparky. "All last night I was praying you'd come back, but if I'd only known what you'd do, I'd have gone into hiding. Git! Get away from me! I'm choking to death."

Gin was thinking that Sparky had no idea how much worse he'd smelled at first but decided he'd go quietly back down to the ocean for a bit and try and soak some of the stink away. So much for the boss's gratitude for his return.

Chapter 23: Mabon, Joe Sam, and Luke New Moon

Mabon and Joe Sam reluctantly left Nora and the others and set out on their quest for the two remaining raiders. The three recent captives, who were now willingly travelling back to camp with Nora and her searchers to their critical meeting with the forest people, had suggested Mabon and the others head back along following the route the three had come up, heading gradually toward the ocean, keeping near to the shore.

They described the area around the sea cave from which they'd fled and guessed it was only a few short hours away. Luke New Moon said he knew of such a cave and volunteered to join them as an elder representing the chief and her village. Luke also explained he wanted to join Mabon's party, especially because two of his sons had married and were living in the area that had been attacked by the outsiders with the guns. He hadn't heard from either of his sons for many months. He couldn't wait to get his hands on the culprits in the cave.

Joe Sam had no trouble picking up signs of the trail to the cave, as it was obvious Earl, Pipes, and Watts had taken no great care to hide evidence of their journey. Mabon invited Luke New Moon to walk along with him behind the trackers, who occasionally paused where the ground was particularly rocky and bare. There were no signs to be picked up there, except an occasional scuffing mark in some patch of sand or clay. But they quickly found more bruised foliage, or broken weeds or branches nearby, and their party was off again.

"What was the last message you got from your boys?" asked Mabon at one point as they were nearing the ocean. They could already hear not-too-distant pounding surf and the occasional shrieks of hungry gulls and other seabirds flying in crisscrossing patterns overhead, their voices calling to one another in high-pitched excitement from the bright blue sunlit sky overhead.

"My oldest boy, Peter, wrote about the attacks on two neighbouring communities. He knew one of the people injured, an elderly woman who approached the invaders in the dark of night. She was shot as she came out to investigate what she thought were flames coming from the community meeting shelter. She said there were maybe six or seven of them, all outsiders, and there were at least three guns. She never got to describe them properly, because they ran away after the gunshot and she was very weak. She was carried into safe shelter where she could be cared for in relative safety.

"The younger one hasn't written for many weeks. His last letter told of his new babies, twin girls who looked like their mother." He paused and stopped walking and whispered, "We are close to shore now and not far from the cave we are seeking. It will be wiser to approach the cave by the shore if the tide allows."

"Let's find out," said Mabon. He ran ahead to speak to the trackers and tell them his intentions. They turned and agreed to approach the shore and maintain silence until they were certain where the two gunmen were hiding.

The tide was out far enough to allow them to travel on the dry sand close to the shelter of the high banks once they climbed gingerly down the steep bank. Luke had led them to a crumbled bit of cliff where the broken stones formed a natural stair leading down to the gravel and pebbles at the bottom and onto the warm sand.

Slowly they made their way along the cliffs in single file, the only sounds coming from gulls and other screaming birds overhead, the crunching of the sand or pebbles underfoot, the steady, regular lapping of the waves against sand and pebbles and the constant sea breeze brushing in against the land.

"Not far now," said Luke in a loud whisper. "We will be able to see the beach just under the caves and the stream that pours in and out of the cave from the sea. All is quiet now, but in stormy weather the waves break on the cave entrance like the rolling of thunder and the rock base of the land all around here shakes with the crash of each giant wave."

"Luke and I will move around the point and make sure the way is clear," said Mabon. The others nodded and willingly sat down on a huge, dry driftwood log that had likely been lifted onto the shore during a recent autumn storm and settled with the help of wind and wave to its secure position in the sand. It provided a secure and somewhat comfortable resting place.

"Shhh," whispered Luke as he peered around the jutting rock of the point. He gestured for Mabon to come up beside him, and with a smile, he pointed at something down by what must be the stream leading inside the massive cave. There appeared to be someone sitting on top of a large, flat-topped stone, sunning himself, and he didn't appear to be wearing many clothes.

"What do we do now?" asked Luke.

Mabon squinted in the reflection of low sun off the ocean water. He scanned the area near the rock platform where the figure sat, and as he and Luke drew nearer, he could make out a few scattered articles of clothing drying in the sun. He wondered about a gun. He saw no sign of one, but knew he couldn't be certain from this distance with the low sun in his eyes.

"Wait here," said Mabon. "I'm going to try and get closer. If I give you a big wave, come and bring the others with you. If I don't wave, stay put."

Mabon made his way up along the ocean cliff, keeping to the shadows as best he could. He reasoned that even if the near-naked man on the rock turned toward him, the man would have real difficulty detecting a human presence against the shaded face of the cliff.

Soon he found himself about twenty metres away from his prey and he could clearly smell a strong wild smell, like a male fox or perhaps even a skunk. The smell had been getting stronger as he approached the man. From here the former Ranger could see that the man was wearing only what once must have been white underwear.

As Mabon made his decision to run to the man and take him down off the rock, his quarry suddenly jumped off his perch and quickly gathered up his clothes. He took his belongings in his arms and waded through the stream easily, as it was apparently no more than a metre deep. The man quickly disappeared behind the rocks on the other side. Mabon stood and waved his arms and waited as his trackers came around the distant rocks and ran as quickly as they could toward him.

As his party of trackers approached him, he realized he wasn't certain whether he had been seen by the naked man. He decided that for everyone's safety, they would lie low for a few hours before attempting a raid on the cave. He told his crew the naked man had almost certainly been sprayed by a skunk and had likely come to the sea in order to wash up and get rid of the horrid stink.

Mabon suggested they all return to their shelter under the riverbank and get a bit of rest, and wait for complete darkness or perhaps morning before they try to capture whoever was sheltering inside.

By now he was quite sure the naked man hadn't seen him as he approached the big rock. His jumping down from the rock and running across the shallow stream had merely been coincidental. They would await the cover of darkness and let their prey get to sleep before doing anything. They had no guns, and approaching their prey even in the failing daylight would be too dangerous. Especially if the nearly naked man had seen them and given warning.

Chapter 24:
Emergency Visit

Adam and Paul were breathing heavily and feeling exhausted as they approached the shoreline. The light had begun to fade into the evening. Darkness never really comes under a cloudless sky when one lives mostly outdoors. The two young men had been travelling, sometimes running for what seemed many hours now, and they hoped they hadn't bypassed Mabon and his party of searchers or missed any action or excitement.

The youngsters were worried about Alice and her sickness, knowing it was serious because of the hasty turnaround that Nora and Blanchfleur had suggested, and the fact the youngsters had been sent out into who knew what dangers. But secretly, the young men were excited about being out where they might have a hand in this present adventure.

Adam and Tish and Nora and the others, including Pipes, Earl, and Watts and only excluding

Mabon, Joe Sam, and Luke, had arrived at the settlers' camp, and had no sooner settled their three captors into temporary quarters then they learned that Tish's mother had been taken gravely ill. Blanchfleur and Tish and the elderly medicine woman from the forest people's village were taking good care of Alice and doing the best they could, but the former mayor was worried about her daughter.

She wanted Mabon to return with his bag of medicines and his knowledge as soon as possible. She appreciated the efforts of the medicine woman that Kate, the chief, had sent along from the forest people village, but she had learned to become more comfortable and reliant on Mabon and his skill. Adam was ready to go at once, but Blanchfleur insisted he not go alone, so it was quickly arranged for Paul, the son of the chief, to join him.

"Can Tish come with us?" said Adam.

Tish looked at him with uncertainty, and then at the small house where she lived, and where her ill mother lay in an uncertain state. "I'd like that," she said, "but I should stay here with my mother and grandmother. They both need me now. But hurry back as soon as you can, and be careful," she said, trying her best not to look worried and more than a bit jealous, but mostly feeling conflicted and worried to bits.

"Do you know where you're going to find them?" asked Blanchfleur.

"Those guys talked about a sea cave," said Adam.

"I know where that cave is," said Paul. "It is said to be an old, abandoned gold mine from times long past. My father and uncles and brothers and I slept in it one rainy night on a fishing trip when I was a kid."

"Can you find it again?" asked Adam.

"Yes, I know exactly how to get there, and by the shortest route," he said.

After a few more cautions to be careful, the two boys gathered up a few supplies and headed out on the run. They hoped to catch up with Mabon and Nora and Luke New Moon before the adults reached the cave, but they soon realized it wasn't going to be possible to catch up unless the grownups stopped somewhere. Both Adam and Paul hoped they could catch them up ahead before they captured their quarry and had turned for home. They wanted the best for Alice, but they wanted to also be in on the adventure of a lifetime.

They soon began to see scattered fragments of moonlight between the branches of shoreline trees as they bounced off the surface of the ocean surf before they arrived the top of the steep, rocky cliff that Paul had described and spotted the worn, gravelled pathway that led down to the shore. The pathway looked steep enough to pose them problems, but they didn't see a better way. They were partway down when Paul suddenly stumbled and fell, letting out a surprised, pinched-off squeak, which was the best he could do to suppress his stunned surprise at falling and rolling down the slippery, dew-coated pebbles.

Chapter 25: Reunion

As Mabon and his search party returned to the place near the large log where their gear was stored, they heard Paul's accidental yelp and the staccato rattle of disturbed pebbles and another startled outcry as the chief's son landed on the sandy beach with a solid thud. Mabon signalled everyone to crouch on the pebbled sand underfoot until they found out who or what had tumbled down the rocky bank so close to their temporary camp. Was it one of the armed killers from the cave? Was their prey on to their presence? Had the near-naked man actually seen Mabon or any of them?

They waited motionless a few minutes in absolute silence. No one wanted to be the murderer's next victim. Then there was a young voice speaking and Mabon recognized Adam at once. What was his son doing here?

"Adam," he whispered in his quietest voice. "Is that you? Are you alone? What on earth are you doing here?"

Adam heard the beloved voice of his dad. And the whisper was a sure signal that they should maintain silence. He helped his companion, Paul, to his feet as he said quietly to his father, "Yes, and Paul is here with me." He said nothing more until he and Paul stood in front of the big former Ranger. Mabon held his gaze and waited. Adam's serious expression told him the young men were here on an important errand.

Adam swallowed hard and spoke, "Alice is very sick. They want you and your medicine bag at once."

Mabon explained the urgency of their present situation concerning the outlaws in the cave and described the appearance of a naked man who reeked of skunk, who had been on the beach by the cave just up ahead. He said that they would rest until they were sure their quarry was asleep, and then they would check out the cave, and whether they managed to capture their prey or not, he and some of the party would leave immediately for home. Adam and Paul would return with him.

Mabon and his team believed that the two killers would probably still be in the cave, and whoever they found there would be armed and dangerous and had at very least one gun and some ammunition. Mabon and some of his party would capture them tomorrow and take them prisoner. Adam and the boys would be sent back to camp to help the stricken Alice.

"Come with me, Adam," said Mabon. "We'll find you and Paul a place to sleep; you must be beat."

"Don't worry about us. Paul and I have our own bedding and gear close by, and we'll be all right. See you in the morning," he said, feeling confident and strong. He remembered the long-ago battle back when he was a mere child, when the old ones had been attacked back in the Happy Valley.

Those were hard times, but sometimes he remembered how he had felt more grown up back then than he did recently, and that was such a long time ago. Life in the old camp divided adults from the young, and he felt that he'd lost something important when he was no longer considered useful.

But his and Tish's capture by the kidnappers and this trip travelling along with Paul had given him back his old confidence and feeling of self-reliance.

He was almost asleep and nearing a dream state when he was startled by Paul's whisper.

"I have an idea," said his friend and fellow adventurer. "Get up and come with me."

Adam sleepily crawled out from under his

warm blankets, shivering. He was wearing a woollen sweater and a pair of heavy cloth pants that had been handed down from some unknown stranger from the distant past. Often the forest people harvested tons of old clothes they gathered from the ruins of old store buildings in abandoned towns and villages scattered about the forest.

"Come on!" whispered Paul.

Adam looked around him; it appeared everyone else was resting. He wondered how they could rest with all the excitement. Some were breathing softly, while others made a variety of snoring sounds as waves lapped in a soothing pattern against the pebbled and sandy shore. The tide had risen much closer to their gear than it had been when they had lain down for the night. There was someone standing watch on the cliff above and they could see his outline against the starlit sky. They would have to move quietly so as not to be noticed.

"Where are we going?" he whispered sleepily and had yawned again as he hurried along behind his taller friend.

"You'll see," said Paul. "I have an idea." He picked up speed and Adam followed as they moved as stealthily as possible up the cool sand of the beach in the direction of the cave.

"Tell me," said Adam, hurrying to keep up. He was almost running beside his friend as Paul explained: "When I last camped in the cave up ahead with my uncle and the others, I swam in and out of the cave to the ocean on a night just like this one. I bet those two galoots are sleeping in the cave, and I want to prove to you that I'm not always clumsy and falling down on the side of cliffs. We could climb the path up the cliff on the other side of the inlet, but that's probably how those men come and go; they may have a guard on lookout."

"You're not thinking of swimming in there when they have guns, are you?" He punched Paul lightly on his muscled arm.

Paul chuckled. "Not exactly. I was thinking that we'll both go in, and I'll climb up to the dry ledge where they probably are. You can watch and signal me if they wake up. I can move very slowly; the way my uncles taught me to make myself invisible when we were hunting our winter's meat. Are you a good swimmer?"

"Yes, Grandfather Ueland taught me how to swim in his pool at the Manuhome. He swam every morning and night. I can swim okay. But I'm not so sure it's wise to swim into that cave."

"You're not afraid, are you?" Paul asked, the distant moon lighting his sly smile.

"A little," said Adam. "Do you really think we should do it?" He was just a bit afraid but also excited at the thought of sneaking into the cave.

He wondered if Paul really thought he could make himself invisible.

"I know we should. When I swam here, out of the weather and the cold wind, the adults didn't hear me coming in or going out. But even with the sound of the sea, we will have to swim quietly, like two dogs, with no splashing. I will show you where to stand so you can watch, and they won't see you even if they do wake up. I will move all around them like a ghost and I'll take their guns and their bullets, and even some of their food, and maybe their shoes and extra clothes. We'll carry their guns out and toss them into the salt sea with their other things and we'll be back to camp before the others notice we're gone. Do you want to try, or are you scared?"

Adam hesitated only a moment. "Let's do it," he said.

"Even if the cave smells like a rotten skunk?" asked Paul, laughing softly.

"Even if it smells as bad as you," said Adam, and they both suppressed excited laughter.

Paul was still laughing on the inside as they crept in near silence over to the stream where water flowed in and out of the cave, carrying on its back the golden blanket of the moonlight. Adam followed his friend's lead as he removed his soft shoes and all his clothing except his undershorts and they waded into the chilly ocean water and glided into the rank, dusky interior of the sea cave.

Paul stopped and treaded water as he pointed out a series of small steps that someone had previously cut out of the solid granite of the cave interior. Adam, dripping wet, raised himself up so that he could look across at two blanket-covered figures lying inert and snoring on the shelf to their right. The skunk smell was sickening but tolerable.

Paul pulled himself up out of the water slowly, like an unfolding snake, allowing the water to drip silently to the rock under his large feet. He waited only a minute or two, crinkling up his nose, before he circled the sleeping figures in absolute silence, walking gracefully as a large cat on the balls of his feet. He held a single finger in the air, and in one motion picked up a rifle and handed it across to Adam.

Adam had never held a rifle in his hands, and he felt very uncomfortable with it. He worried how he would ever swim out of the cave carrying the awkward weapon.

He had taken his eyes off Paul only for a moment when he turned and noticed that one of the men under the blankets had turned over and grunted as Paul, close beside him, froze into a rigid statue. He stayed motionless for what seemed long minutes but were merely a few anxious seconds, and then began to toss boots and clothing and pots and pans and knives and utensils and containers of bits and pieces of food off the shelf, into the water. He found two boxes of matches and emptied them in a shower of wooden sticks into the seawater and then he waved and slipped silently into the splashing waves. He swam to Adam and reached for the rifle, which he slung across and strapped to his back and swam swiftly and easily out of the cave.

Adam followed and shortly stepped up on the sand outside in the moonlight. The water, he discovered, had been warmer than the air, and now he shivered. He looked around and couldn't see where Paul had gone until he gazed out onto the gold-painted brow of the ocean and saw an arm hold a rifle into the air and fling it even farther out into the deep green, salty water. Adam waited until he returned and decided he was nearly dry enough to dress. He leaned against a large boulder that smelled faintly of skunk and waited for Paul to join him.

They arrived back at the shelter where most of the others still slept and climbed under their blankets long before the first light of morning began to emerge from the horizon, far out on a peaceful sea. They would tell Mabon what they had done in the morning, and the capture of the worst of the most dangerous of the fugitives should be as easy as dropping in for a visit.

Adam learned a great lesson that night. Disarming an enemy was not always a matter of power or violence. It was about silence and knowledge and confidence and courage.

Chapter 26: The Most Violent of Enemies

Mabon and his company of adventurers arrived at the top of the cliff after crossing the stream, which had returned to a morning low tide. Adam and Luke and his entire crew entered the cave to find both of their violent enemies at one another's throats, yelling and striking at one another and blaming each other for what had happened to their weapon, their scarce ammo, and their other supplies.

Mabon's sharp voice startled them into silence, and they sat in dirty T-shirts and ragged underpants on top of their blankets, the only possessions they were able to discover upon waking up.

They were out-powered and outnumbered and lacking in alternatives to marching peacefully along beside their captors and worrying what evils would be coming their way because of their stupid, inhumane activities. The complete company marched swiftly on empty stomachs toward the home camp, where Mabon and his medicine bag were needed at once.

Adam and Paul couldn't take their eyes off the two feared enemies, who now looked pathetic and terrified and weak, and they wondered how anyone could have been afraid of either of them. And yet they knew. Any gutless, despicable creature can ruin the lives of the most powerful of his neighbours if they are given free access to murderous weapons and not given a proper education and the chance to experience real love and compassion.

Adam caught Paul's eye, and after another glance at their pathetic prisoners, they shook their heads in disbelief and felt thankful for the communities they lived in and the beautiful people they lived among.

Adam was feeling a repressed kind of excitement after the adventure with Paul in the sea cave. He kept shaking his head and looking first at Paul and then at Mabon and the latest prisoners.

In many ways, the whole episode seemed like a dream. And at the same time, he had been surprised that nothing had been said by the adults about their adventure having been foolhardy and dangerous. He had expected at least a comment to that effect, or perhaps some downright anger, but no one had voiced anything of the sort.

Perhaps it was the urgency of getting to the cave before their quarry could get organized enough to flee. But here they were on their way back to camp with the two scoundrels in tow, and it had been he and Paul who had made the swift conclusion of the event possible, even safe and easy.

He couldn't help smiling and feeling pride, but he still knew that he hadn't necessarily heard the end of the episode.

Chapter 27:
More Questions
than Answers

There was great excitement around the settlers' homesteads as word spread from village to village and for long miles in all directions. Visitors came from near and far to have a look at all the new arrivals, the growing awareness of the possibly goodly number of survivors from the Aahimsa Manuhome, its factories and farmlands. But many of these more recent visitors came to have a look at the pathetic disarmed monsters who had terrorized the whole region with their bullets and fires.

Mostly the ones who came to look were relieved and curious. But there were those among them whose hearts came seeking revenge and atonement upon the evil men who burned their homes and farmlands and who even may have killed their elders and their families and their children. It became quickly obvious that this latest pair would have to be dealt with in a much more serious manner than the others.

Adam had been pleased to learn that Alice had responded well to the healers of the forest people and had begun to improve in her health only a few hours after Adam and Paul had left to fetch Mabon and his skill and medicine bag home. When they arrived with their captives in tow, Tish's mother was smiling and on her feet among the welcoming crowds.

Word of the success of the mission had preceded them, as Luke New Moon had sent a swift runner ahead of the party, and a few of the elders and the youth from the forest people's village stood close behind Alice and Tish and Nora.

Adam enjoyed the welcome, especially the enthusiastic hugs from Alice and his mother and even Blanchfleur. Tish had stood in the background and approached him shyly and they, too, had an awkward but not unpleasant hug.

A large crowd gathered as the two captives, nearly naked and filthy, were taken to one of the empty wigwams. It was one of the older shelters that was mostly used for winter storage of summer articles and extra non-perishable supplies that didn't need to be stored in the cooler underground rock and clay shelters, which were more secure holding places for anyone who must be detained.

But it was decided these two foul-smelling prisoners would be held above ground. The fact that they still reeked of skunk made the job of finding volunteers to guard them difficult. In the end, they were snugly tied and fettered, and they slept in their temporary quarters with a ring of volunteers standing vigilantly on guard outside the perimeter of the wigwam.

Adam slept well that night in the company of both his beloved parents, Nora and Mabon, and his friend, Paul. The story of what the two boys had accomplished spread far and wide, despite the efforts of Mabon and Nora to keep it quiet. And when the forest people's chief and the council invited Paul and Adam to take part in the gathering that would decide the fate of the latest scoundrels, the adults, after a long discussion, decided it would be fine, even though everyone in all the combined camps knew that this would be no ordinary council, as attempted murder and arson were not charges that had been dealt with for many years.

Adam had crazy dreams that night, swimming in and out of the cave with Paul while a trial took place inside with the two prisoners tied together to a wooden post that sat atop a tall mound of wooden firewood, and the forest people stood before them holding burning torches and shouting and screaming in angry voices at the prisoners, who were cringing and crying out for mercy with piteous looks on their faces and tears streaming from their eyes.

He awoke several times and tried to get back to dreamless sleep, but the bad dream kept returning until he got up and walked around the camp, stopping to observe the spot where a dozen elders from the forest people calmly kept guard over the prisoners. He asked to look inside, and he was permitted a quick look. He saw the prisoners tied to one another and a large chunk of iron, dozing like two stinking and oversized babies, and he returned to his sleeping family and within minutes fell fast asleep.

Chapter 28: The Circle

Adam sat beside Tish and her mother, Alice, among the elders of the forest people watching as the chief and Nora and Mabon invited the prisoners to sit on round chunks of maple facing the whole of the gathered crowd. Earlier the prisoners had been stripped and scrubbed clean by the forest people's oldest members, who had experience with cleaning up every messy child in the forest around and of every stray dog or human who stumbled on and scared any number of the black-and-white skunks that marched about after dark seeking grubs and insects. Most of the grime and filth that had separated criminals and people visually had been removed, and they now resembled any pair of frightened children in the presence of angry parents.

The chief was the first to address the prisoners and the gathering crowd, which had been steadily growing and noisily discussing the spectacle before them, but now fell silent as the chief raised her arms high into the sky.

"We who share this forest arrive this morning knowing of many historical systems of law and order that could be applied to the charges against the two scoundrels, who by their own admission have committed serious crimes against our people. Systems of justice have existed in this place going far into the past, long before ships came bearing the written teachings of European and Asian cultures. Our Indigenous traditions existed for centuries before "civilization" came and worked to destroy the heritage and culture of this widely populated and civilized new world. Our system focused on stabilizing society, its goal to restore the justice that had been tampered with. It did not exist merely to punish or to take revenge, but for one type of crime, the crimes of murder or attempted murder. For these it gave the rights and responsibility to the families of the murdered or wounded person to seek justice from the offender who inflicted injury or violence against a loved one.

"That was what was. But until today, we have not for a very long time needed such severe and unforgiving punishment. The European settlers came with their guns and diseases and their traditions of jailing prisoners and handing out punishments that only led to more retaliation and revenge and on and on. We do not want those times to return. I hope we can find ways to deal with the criminals here before us to allow them to learn and grow, to change and become useful to themselves and others.

"We hope for this, but we cannot allow such serious crimes against our people as these to be repeated.

"We must use our hearts and our minds to attempt to heal these people and those whose lives and security have been harmed by their actions. So, let us begin. Are there people here who have lost loved ones or property due to the actions of the two accused?"

About a dozen of the onlookers stood and raised their arms.

"Please come down front and seat yourselves outside the circle but around the prisoners. Do not speak to them or touch them. It is important for all of you to be together for healing to take place and reconciliation to begin."

Eleven fierce-looking forest people, complete strangers to the local population, who had huddled together upon arrival, scrambled down from the upper part of the lakeside bank and settled down in the thick green grass surrounding the maple logs where the prisoners sat. One of the accused, the tall, thin one who called himself Gin, looked around quickly and began to whimper dolefully.

The two prisoners waited, their faces grim and uncertain, having no notion as to what would come next. Both looked away from their accusers and kept their eyes fixed on the ground, afraid to look directly at anyone in the large crowd, or the relatives of the victims, or even at one another.

The chief rose and Adam and the other settler village representatives, along with the elders from nearby forest people's villages, also stood and formed a circle around Gin and Sparky, and all but the prisoners knew that the hearing was about to begin.

"You know why we have brought you to this place?" the chief asked. The two prisoners did not look up or respond in any way, except for the pathetic, loud whimpering that continued from the mouth of the tall one. The chief stepped closer to the two men and they looked up at her with fear in their eyes.

"Did you hear the question?" she repeated.

They both nodded.

"Explain it to us," she said.

"We're sorry," said the second man, the one they called Sparky.

"Sorry for what?" asked the chief.

The two looked at one another and stayed silent.

Mabon stood up at this point.

"May I speak?" he asked. The chief nodded, and Mabon began.

"This hearing won't work unless you are willing to talk the truth to us. If you can talk to us with trust and honesty, we may be able to help you and still render justice to those you have harmed. If you can't, we will do what we are required, and turn you over to our visitors from the injured families. If they take you, the families of the injured have the right to judge and punish you. If you cooperate, you may be able to remain here in safety under certain strict rules we agree on. It is up to you. If you remain silent, you will be handed over and the hearing is over. There will be nothing more we can do to help you."

"What are the conditions?" asked Sparky.

Mabon sat and Kate rose from her seat at the top of the circle. "There are few conditions beyond what has been spoken by our friend, Mabon, who brought his people to this forest a few years back. His people came to us looking for new lives where they could live in peace and safety.

"It is that peace and safety we seek at this gathering of interested friends and neighbours. Mabon and his people came here looking for new lives, and we offered a share of our lives and ourselves in honesty and in trust. We will be asking you to trust us to judge whether you might be able to tell us about your lives and how you came to be the way you are, and to act the way you have acted. We in the circle will try to help you in your quest for justice and in our quest for justice and security. You must tell us why you think and act the way you do, and prove to us that you are fit to live in peace among us. If you satisfy the circle, and the crowds gathered here outside the circle, that you are opening your hearts and minds to change, and if you promise that you will not act in such evil and mindless ways again, we may decide you can become a part of our communities. And you can redeem yourselves to the community by becoming useful and loyal parts of all our lives here in Creator's forest."

"Are you ready to begin?" asked a voice in the crowd. All heads turned toward the woman who sat among the group of strangers whose family members had been injured and whose homes were damaged or destroyed, and then to the two pathetic-looking subjects of this reconciliation gathering.

"We are," said Kate. "I would like to introduce you to two courageous people among the many people of courage who surround you. They are both young men who used their minds and their hearts to help capture you without causing further harm to our people and to yourselves. They swam into your hiding place and removed your weapons and your clothing and left you unarmed, in fear, and helpless, without harming a hair on your heads. When they come forward to ask you a few questions to begin, I want you both to thank them for your lives and the chance at having much better lives in the future."

Kate paused and gestured to her son, Paul, and his best friend, Adam. The two young men stood and moved forward, Adam turning to glance at Mabon and Nora, who smiled proudly at him.

The young men looked at one another a moment and then at the two captives. Paul stared, and his face showed his anger and his scorn. Adam, after looking at his parents sitting side by side, turned to the two men and once again wondered why anyone would have to be afraid of the likes of them. They were weak and pathetic. Paul nodded to Adam and sat. Adam stepped down close enough to touch the two prisoners should he wish to. The nervous men shied away from him.

"I'm sorry," the two nervous prisoners muttered almost together.

"I'm sure you are," said Adam. "Because we caught you and brought you here. Because you lost your gun and your bullets. Because you lost your power over people asleep in their beds. Everyone here already knows you are sorry and why. But we want to know how or why you would want to do the cruel and senseless things that could bring you no happiness and only injure and terrify innocent strangers.

"We want you to tell us about yourselves. We need to understand how two grown men could behave as you were behaving. We already know what you did. But we need to hear you tell us what you did out loud, so you can hear it for yourselves and know the serious nature of the things you did. Then we want to hear from those who might have lost loved ones or had family harmed, or friends or neighbours, and how much your behaviour hurt them. Then we want you to tell us about your lives. What was it about your lives that could allow you to act the way you have acted?"

Adam paused and looked at Paul. "This is the brave person who you must thank for saving you. Paul had the courage to walk among you as you were sleeping and take away your weapon. You might have woken and injured or killed him. But he walked through your sleep and protected you and our people from your evil spirits. He could have hurt you or ended your lives and this circle would not be taking place. You owe him. So, listen to him." He gestured for Paul to come forward and dropped into Paul's vacant space, where he sat quietly.

Paul moved closer to the men. "It will soon be your chance to speak and to tell us everything about your lives so we may try to understand and guide you to better ways. It will help us to know how we can guide you and teach you to lose the anger or the confusion that allows you do what you have done. If you are not able to do that, we will turn your fate over to the injured ones, and they will take you away or leave you here for us to punish. In the end you will decide whether you live with us in peace.

"Or, we will take you one at a time to a place where you will be by yourself in the wildest part of the forest, far from here, where you will be left on your own, a stranger among the forest and its creatures, and its spirits, who will decide your fate.

"You will have nothing but your bare hands and your courage and knowledge to help you. If it is decided at this council that you are worth keeping, you will have the help and the guidance of the elders, and all the people of the forest, new settlers and old First Nation. It is our wish that you accept the gift being offered to you and that you change your ways and before long become yourselves a gift to the people."

Paul rose and dropped down beside Adam. Kate gestured to one of the elders in the circle, who rose and faced the men.

The old woman rose slowly, as she was the oldest among all the elders and the mother and grandmother of a large family. She was much honoured and beloved among the forest people for her generosity and wisdom.

"I have lost children to anger and fighting but never to senseless acts like you two creatures carried out. My heart aches for the losses you have caused to our neighbours and the terror and fear that you set loose upon the whole people of the forest. I want to hear from you now." She pointed a long, thin finger at Gin, who continued to look down at his bare feet.

Gin began to whimper again. The old woman raised her voice and stepped with vigor toward the prisoners. "Stop that ugly noise and spare me the blubbering. What are you, babies? Children? And speak to us in clear voices. And speak out from your heart if you have one," she said.

Gin raised his head and said, "I'm sorry."

"No, you're not sorry. You don't even know what you have done. Tell us what you have been doing."

"I've been bad. I hurt people."

"What did you do?"

"I shot at people," he said.

"Did your bullets hit anyone?"

Gin lowered his head and looked terrified.

"How many?" she continued.

"I don't know," he said, tears running down his face.

"Did you hurt people?" she asked.

"Yes," he said.

"Did you try to help any of them?" she asked, her voice losing much of its intensity.

"No," Gin said. "I was afraid of them."

"Did any of them die?" she asked.

"I don't know," he said.

"What else did you do?" she asked.

"We set villages on fire," he said.

"Why?" she asked.

"So we could escape," he said. By now he had stopped crying.

"What else did you do?"

"We stole food and clothing and things we needed," he said.

"But those things weren't yours." She paused. "If you had asked for help, things would have been given to you." She paused a moment and began again. "Have you ever watched anyone die?"

"No."

"Anyone you loved ever die?" she said. "It's a terrible thing to watch when someone you love dies." She gestured to the visitors outside the circle. "Some of these people saw families and friends that you shot almost die. Any idea how that would feel?"

"No, I have no family or friends, and I never saw anyone die. Nobody at the Manuhome ever died, they were taken away by the Rangers when they got old and useless. I was brought there as a boy to work, and I worked all my life. They operated on all of us, so we couldn't ever be fathers. I was angry, and I didn't get along with others. They put me in worse and worse places in the Manuhome because I was bad, until they put me down in hell with the heater pipes. Everybody down there called the heating pipe area 'hell.' When I got out of hell just before the Manuhome blew up, I was angrier than I ever was before, and I did bad things, and I don't know why, and I'm sorry. I didn't have anything to live for. I think I was hoping someone would kill me, even though I was scared to die, but they never did. I'm always scared. I want to learn to be better, if I have a chance to learn."

Kate rose then and held up one hand, open-palmed, toward Gin's face, which seemed more peaceful than before for having spoken. The chief, too, seemed satisfied for now. She signalled for Gin to sit and for Sparky to stand. Sparky lifted his large frame up and stood, almost quaking before the crowd, which had begun to murmur like swirling grackles, the sound coming in almost musical waves of interchanging sounds and silence. Kate felt the reaction was a good sign; for the first time, her people felt at least a small portion of sympathy for the unfortunate Gin.

She turned her hard eyes on Sparky.

"It is your turn," she said. "Is your story the same as this man's?" she asked and waited.

"Part of it," he began. "We both had no parents and only knew how to work. We were slaves who learned to do the jobs we were given. I got into trouble soon after I arrived in the Manuhome by setting fire to the dormitory where I slept with other young workers. Like me, these workers were sent from the donor's temple in the city to do the jobs of the old ones who were terminated.

"The other workers didn't like me and picked on me. I was sent to sweat in hell by Ueland after the fire when I was only nine years old. I worked in greasy filth and heat every day of my childhood until I took a course and was put in charge of ceramic pipe repairs. Then I had a day off to sleep in my own space a few days a month. Like Gin, I had no fun, no friends, no adventure in my life until the day of the explosion, when we walked along Ueland's rails behind the very last trains that abandoned us and we escaped.

"I didn't know anything about looking after myself and I went crazy looking for excitement and some way to stay alive in a new and terrifying world I did not understand. Like Gin, I had no family ever, no one to teach me or look out for me. Only hot, boring work and pain and hopelessness." Then the killer called Sparky sat and hung his head, and he wept like a child.

Elsewhere there was silence. The only sound was the two grown villains weeping and saying over and over that they were sorry. Kate rose and faced the crowd, which sat almost as if frozen in time.

"It is difficult to absorb and understand the forces that drive a hated enemy." The sound of the pathetic murmuring and childlike weeping echoed across the still, chill water of the lake and deep into the cold darkness of the forest.

She gestured to the crowd to rise and they did, slowly, their legs stiff from sitting, their minds churning over the absurd behaviour of these brutal criminals reduced to blubbering children before their eyes.

"We will stop now and sleep on this. Tomorrow we will meet here again, and we will hear from all the families and friends who have suffered loss. Some of these suffering ones are just now arriving or about to arrive. I hope those of us here will share what we've heard today with the newcomers and will return to hear from the many victims directly and indirectly injured by these men. Go now and rest."

She turned to the appointed guardians of the prisoners and nodded while the weeping, pitiful duo marched together back to their temporary quarters to wait for the late morning, when the fateful hearing would continue.

Chapter 29: Late-Night Conversations

This night Adam and Paul and Tish had been invited to join the elders who had been chosen to guard the prisoners. There were six warrior elders and two of the younger hunters and trackers who formed a ring around the large wigwam. Mabon, Joe Sam, Nora, and two elders were on the inside in a line that separated the exit and the prisoners. Adam, Paul, and Tish were allowed inside the shelter, and they arranged themselves in their sleeping blankets close to the adults. The prisoners were tied together, their legs spread apart at the ankles by two peeled branches of elm with Vs at each end that kept their feet wide apart and made it impossible to walk or run, or even to stand up without support.

"Their legs look like slingshots," Adam whispered. Paul laughed. Tish gave the boys a confused look. Paul mimicked someone using a slingshot, stretching the tight string and releasing the imaginary stone at an imaginary target. Tish smiled.

"Are they asleep?" she whispered.

Adam shook his head.

"They look scared," she whispered again.

"Shhh!" said Nora. "Try to sleep."

Adam and Paul were soon dozing beside the adults, all of whom slept but Nora and Mabon. Tish used every trick she knew to fall asleep but couldn't seem to manage.

After a long time in the dark, as the fire in the wigwam's centre faded to smoky coals, she heard one of the prisoners whispering to himself.

"I'm scared. What are they going to do to us? Will they burn us like we burnt the villages, or will they kill us for revenge?" There was silence for a short while and Tish was almost asleep when she heard what she guessed was the same man crying. She assumed it was the tall skinny one called Gin.

"They are trying not to do bad things to you," she said. "They are trying to find out if you could change and then be able to live with us and not hurt us," she said. She wasn't sure Gin had heard her, but he stopped crying and she was glad. It made her sad when he cried. Even if he was a bad person. She wondered if he would say anything, even if he had heard her. A few moments later she thought she heard a faint voice. She waited again.

"Do you really mean that?" asked the voice timidly. Tess heard Mabon turn in his sleeping blankets amid the deep breathing of the others and the soft snoring of a few.

"Mean what?" she whispered as softly as she could manage.

"That they might not punish us?" Gin (she was sure it was Gin) said.

"There will be some sort of punishment. But it will be doing a useful job like everyone else. Doing work that will help others, everyone in the community. These people do not want revenge. They want to fix you. But they know that not everyone can be fixed, and not everyone wants to be fixed. If you can't be fixed, they take you out where the wild dogs and the bears can find you. You will have to find a way to live alone. If you speak the truth and you listen and do your best, you can live with all of us as your family. This is what the forest people have taught us, and this is how we are learning to live together and serve one another."

"Is this true? Is it possible?" asked Gin. His voice was quiet now, as if filling with hope. "But you are only a child. Can this be true?"

Mabon's deep, powerful voice came now, loud and clear.

"She is a child. But she speaks the truth. The forest people have taught us what we already knew but were never allowed to live before. We were 'civilized.' We believed that justice could be found in punishment and revenge even when we spoke of love. We believed we could use warriors and armies to bring peace, but armies and battles brought only more hate and more war. We believe now that we can only have peace and justice if we learn from one another and understand why some people do wrong, that previous wrongs grow new generations of wrong. Listen to this child. Listen and learn and your life can begin again with a new direction and you can know how a family can live in peace and love."

Tess looked around and realized that everyone in the wigwam was awake and had been listening to her, and she knew that she had listened to an enemy and spoken words of peace from her heart. She looked over at Adam and realized that he too had been listening, and he and Paul agreed with every word and they looked happy. Both young men smiled at her and nodded their approval.

Tess slipped down happily into her sleeping blankets and soon she and all around her, prisoners and watchers alike, were soundly asleep.

Chapter 30: A Journey to the Unknown

The circle of truth and reconciliation ended well. Gin and Sparky were given a year to try out a new life and prove their trustworthiness. They were given responsibilities over the lighting of the morning fires and the gathering of wood and water from the lake and the surrounding forest. It took them a few weeks to control their enthusiasm and to limit the number and intensity of the fires, but through time they became the best of all the providers of fire and water to both the settlers' community and the forest peoples.

One evening around one of those fires, a discussion began between Blanchfleur and Alice that soon was joined by Nora, Adam, Tish, and Mabon. It all began in answer to a question from Tish, who always seemed to come up with provocative and interesting questions.

"I wonder what has been happening to the other cities like Aahimsa. Were any of the others destroyed?"

Blanchfleur was taken aback by the question. She, too, used to spend much of her spare moments pondering what was taking place in cities around the planet. Then the many responsibilities they all shared within their happy and peaceful community had little by little reduced her curiosity and concerns about the wider world. This question from her granddaughter brought the curiosity screaming back.

"Yes, I wonder, too. There has been no sign of the surveillance we used to expect as normal, and our people have almost forgotten the need to keep out of sight of the eyes in the sky. This is curious indeed. Let me think about it and perhaps we can find a way to answer your question." Blanchfleur watched Tish's pretty face and noted that her granddaughter was intently focused on Adam's reaction to her words. The boy had been juggling three pebbles while he listened to Tish's question and then Blanchfleur's response. He stopped and tossed each of the round stones far into the nearby trees. Then he rose as his friend, Paul, appeared out of those same trees.

"You missed," he said to Adam with a large grin and sat between Adam and Tish.

"Sorry," said Adam, sitting down beside his two friends. "Did you hear Tish's question?"

"I did," he said.

"Were you snooping on us?" asked Tess.

Paul laughed. "Not really," he said. "Your voices go a long way near the water, and I heard the question and Blanchfleur's answer. I think we should form a search party and check out the nearest city. How far away is it? I wouldn't mind going to explore if anyone else is interested."

"Me, too," said Tish. "If anyone is going, I want to go, too."

Blanchfleur stood then, barely suppressing a groan as her weary bones adjusted. "Don't anyone go anywhere until we get a chance to talk this over in more detail. But I won't forget this talk, and perhaps we can come up with a plan that will work."

Nora and Mabon had sat quietly through all of this discussion and were content to listen with a mixture of amusement and excitement as well as a certain amount of concern and anxiety at the implications for themselves and their children, and indeed the wider community. They decided to wait and see if the discussion turned out to be a mere tempest in a teapot, a fancy that would join the endless list of amusing ideas that never came to be, or perhaps become something more. If so, they would do their part to make it work.

It was soon clear that the idea of a trek to explore the fate of the nearest walled city wasn't about to die out. The topic had become the subject of daily discussion and speculation. Mabon and Nora agreed that careful planning was needed before some impulsive youngsters set out rashly and ignited fresh danger and trouble. The present period of peace and contentment had been hard-won, and it would be foolhardy to ruin it. Clearly, no one knew what might be discovered by such an expedition, and what effect such actions might have on the future happiness and safety of the community. But the idea wasn't about to go away.

As they prepared for sleep one evening, Nora said, "Let's speak to Kate and Blanchfleur and form a small group to make a workable plan to get this done."

Mabon grunted agreement. "Yes, it will have to be carefully planned. We must never forget why we came here and how fortunate we are to have the lives we do." He took Nora in his powerful arms and held her close. "We'll begin in the morning.

For the moment, we'll take advantage of our peace and safety and enjoy another good night's sleep."

Chapter 31: The Excursion Begins

Tish and Adam had attended a meeting of the combined councils and, after a detailed briefing, had presented a set of arguments for and against the excursion that had been agreed upon by Kate and Nora, with input by Mabon and a few others who were selected by the chief and Blanchfleur. The council decided that such a journey might prove useful but suggested that the original forest dwellers should not be seen as involved. Such an outing could be perceived as aggression on the part of people with Indigenous origins. If a few of the newcomers wished to venture out in a peaceful bit of carefully planned travel, that might work, so the council reluctantly gave its guarded support.

The two youngsters' suggestion when they returned was that Mabon and Nora and a few of the newcomer people be involved, and that Sparky and Gin go along to ensure they didn't act up in the village without the guidance of Mabon, who they felt had kept them in order thus far.

At first, both Mabon and Nora objected. It would be foolhardy to set out with Sparky and Gin. Adam and Tish explained there was nervousness among the original forest people caused by the arrival of the workers from the Manuhome. All agreed that Mabon and Nora and Blanchfleur and the others had handled the troublemakers well. The forest people elders trusted and respected most of the newcomers, but they were getting nervous and dreaded a return to the constant uprooting of camps and running from those brutal raids out of the walled cities. But after further discussions with the youngsters, they decided they would like to know what there was to fear from their enemies now and in the future. They would feel better if Mabon led a peaceful group to explore and bring back an assessment of the present situation. They felt that Sparky and Gin, who they described as "the raiders," should not be left behind unsupervised while Mabon and his party were gone.

"Perhaps," Kate said, "this could be a genuine test of their promises and their reliability."

And so they were a party of six when they set out on their adventure. Mabon, Nora, Adam, Tish,

Gin, and Sparky. They carried only a minimum of food, supplies, and hunting knives and bows for hunting food. Gin and Sparky were carrying packs of gear and a bit of food and other supplies and seemed quite cheerful at the prospect of getting briefly away from what had become the regular humdrum of village chores.

The group moved cautiously, staying close to or under the cover of trees as they made their way along to the south. As they were settling down for the night inside the brick ruins of an old abandoned factory, they heard rustling outside, a large animal of sorts. Mabon signalled for silence and stepped outside. He returned in a few minutes, followed by Paul, Kate's son, and a friend of Adam and Tish. Neither spoke for a few moments. Paul was wearing a shirt that Mabon recognized as one of his old ones, and a ragged pair of his blue jeans. No one had seen Paul dressed other than in the fashion of the forest people.

"What are you doing here?" Nora said quietly.

"My mother told me where you were going," he said. "And I told her I was going to catch up with you; she told me the council would not approve of it. I said, 'Someone of the forest people should be there to help and to guide them. I know the area better than any of them. Adam and I disarmed the bandits in the cave. I am going to help them.' That's exactly what I said. My mother asked me if this was because of the girl, and I said no," he continued, looking uncomfortable, perhaps embarrassed.

Tish spoke up. "What girl?"

"Never mind," said Nora. She turned to Paul. "You are here now, Paul. Is it your intention to continue with us?"

"Yes," he said. "If you'll have me."

Tish pulled on Adam's sleeve, her eyes on Paul. He shrugged. "You, I'd guess. That's who the girl was. I think he likes you."

Tish stuck out her tongue at Adam and looked away from Paul. She blushed and felt confused. It took her a long while to fall asleep.

Nothing more was said as they tossed and turned and finally settled into their blankets for the night. Mabon damped down the small fire they had used for cooking their meagre meal of bannock and a few small smoked fish.

They were soon asleep. Adam awoke to what sounded like a few giant mosquitoes somewhere outside. A tiny device with a small blue light entered the space and hovered above them and then flitted overhead a few moments before disappearing back outside and fading rapidly into the distance. Adam considered waking the others but realized it would certainly cause a disturbance, and so he decided it could wait for morning.

During the next few minutes Adam noticed how Tish continued to toss and turn beneath her blanket. He thought about how much he had come to like her. He really cared for her, and he was acutely aware that Paul did, too. He wished he knew if she liked him, but thought she probably liked Paul the best, because he was older and braver. That's what he was thinking about when he woke up in the morning, and he remembered he dreamed about her, but he couldn't remember much after the first part.

Nora was awake outside and alone, and she had already started a small fire. She was heating water for tea and mixing water and flour with fat and sea salt to make bannock in an iron skillet. Adam got up and left the tent, then yawned as he stepped quickly to her side and sat. Tish came over then and sat next to him, close. He could hear her teeth chattering.

"I'm cold," she said, shivering and hugging herself as she pulled a buttoned sweater close around her.

He turned and grinned at her. He was cold too, but he felt a kind of unfamiliar warmth at knowing she had decided to sit close beside him. Perhaps she wasn't completely crazy about Paul.

"I heard and saw a drone last night," he said.

"Me, too," said Tish. "First I thought it was a

mosquito or something, and then it got louder and closer and then it came inside. I wasn't sure and didn't want to say anything."

"Me neither," said Adam. "I wonder what it means."

Nora poured batter into the hot skillet and turned to them. "It certainly means something," she said. "We'll have to tell the others. Someone out there knows we are out here and that we're on our way south. We'll have to be very careful over the next while and hope whoever is watching us wishes us no harm. Breakfast will be ready in ten minutes or so. Wake the others and tell them to come and eat. Say nothing about the drones for the moment. We don't want anyone to panic. We'll talk to Mabon and decide whether to continue or to head for safety, or head home. I hope it is still safe."

Nora stayed with the youngsters while they explained what they had seen and heard. The others finished eating and carefully cleaned up as many signs as possible of having camped there. Mabon suggested getting out of sight and waiting a couple of hours to see if anything happened or anyone showed up. Then they told their story to all the others and asked what they thought. It was agreed that there seemed to be no point in turning back now. If they had been seen, then someone or something was aware of their movements. Going home would at best accomplish nothing, and at worst bring some potential harm on the whole settlement.

"Better to carry on and see what, if any, activity is taking place in the nearest city. If we find nothing, we can simply return home and carry on as before. If we discover something, we can warn the others and prepare to move somewhere else in the wild and start over, or take measures to defend ourselves," said Nora. "Do you all agree?"

After a few moments of excited chatter and the expenditure of a lot of nervous energy, everyone agreed to carry on. At this time Sparky approached Adam and Paul, who were helping Tish and Nora get the gear neatly packed for travel.

"Have you seen Gin?" he asked.

The foursome set down their packets and Mabon, who had been on watch nearby, joined them.

"I saw Gin head off into the trees a while ago," the big man said. "I assumed he had private business to take care of. He's been quite a good traveller, doing a good share of the chores. It seems he is turning out to be a cheery companion. But he should have returned by now. I'll have a look."

"We'll come with you," said Tish and the boys. They ran quickly to catch up with Mabon, who stopped suddenly, held up a hand, and signalled them to be silent. "We'll move slowly from here on."

Paul looked concerned and waved his hand to get Mabon's attention. "That would be wise. I smell a bear, a black one, and she's with her cub. If Gin gets too close to them, he could be in real trouble."

Mabon nodded, and they crept forward cautiously, Paul now in the lead. He led them through a set of low, aromatic bay bushes and he signalled them to stop. He pulled back the fragrant branches and they saw that Gin had climbed high up in a spindly birch tree and a huge mountain of black fur was happily trying to shake him off it, like a child shaking ripe apples from an apple tree. Two young baby bears were strolling in the grassy clearing below him, watching their mother play her dangerous game with the terrified Gin and happily romping and play-fighting in the tangled grasses. Tish had to stifle a laugh, as the sight was funny if you weren't aware of the danger in which Gin had found himself.

Paul turned to his friends. "This might seem strange," he said. "But here's what we're going to do. When I count to three, start making as much noise as you can and we'll all run out toward the tree, toward them, yelling all the way. When we get about halfway we'll stop and keep up the noise. She'll probably take her cubs away and run from here."

"Probably?" said Tish.

"What if she doesn't?" asked Adam.

"She probably will," said Mabon, then paused. "We hope."

"Okay, here goes," said Paul, and he let out a series of frightening whoops and ran directly at the huge mother bear. The others followed and began to invent their own best blood-curdling noises. The bear left the tree and turned to them, at first uncertain what was happening, and then, as predicted, ran to her cubs and all three of the dark furry forms rapidly disappeared into the forest.

They were elated, their hearts pounding, as they approached Gin, who squatted on the crumpled long grass, sobbing in terror and moaning, "Thank you, thank you. They were going to eat me. Those bears were trying to eat me. I couldn't hold on much longer." He was wearing an old T-shirt and a pair of worn out long-johns, and his pants were on the ground beside the tree. Mabon picked them up and handed them to him. He was still sobbing and shaking as he pulled them up. "Do you think she would eat me?" he asked, addressing his question to Paul, who had often helped him get acquainted with chores like building the community fires and tidying up. He and the easy-going Paul had become quite friendly.

"If they were hungry, they might kill you and eat you. If she thought you might harm her babies, she would hurt you and perhaps kill you. Usually, though, they avoid people. If they are not hungry, and there are better things in the forest to eat, they would rather be left alone. Sometimes my people would hunt them for their meat or furs. We would sometimes hunt them, and they would sometimes hunt us. That is the way of the wild, the way of the forest and of all her animals."

The friends walked together to rejoin the others, and Gin told them over and over his story of how he had been trapped in a tree by a huge monster of the forest and how his good friends came along just in time to save his life.

Chapter 32:
Many Days of Hard Travel Later

The elders asked Adam and Tish and Paul to take note of and keep a record of any drone or object or aircraft, whether watching them or simply passing overhead. They also asked the others in the party to report anything they had seen or heard to the three youngsters.

They had been travelling away from home for almost a month now and they had not found any sign of a town or a city or even a building that would indicate the presence of a walled city or anything other than a few passive drones that indicated a means of communication or transport.

"This is turning out to be more of an extended camping trip than a reconnaissance of some nearby city's threat," Mabon said to Sparky.

"Nice, though," said Sparky. "Best fun I ever had." He was a strange fellow, this reformed malicious pyromaniac and potential killer. It was hard to believe that he and Gin had been capable of doing the things they were accused of. However, the pair had admitted their wrongdoing and given their accusers a pretty decent understanding of how horrible their lives had been before encountering the traditions and generous justice system of the forest people. Gin and Sparky had found decent lives here in the forest, and a family of sorts, and even the benefit of having children around who would play with them and ask them for help or advice.

"There are so many more of those drones appearing lately than there were," Adam and Tish reported to Mabon. Paul was out foraging for meat and fish while Nora looked around for nuts and berries and fruits and various roots and herbs. Both Nora and Mabon had suggested that everyone not react to their appearance near them or their annoying buzzing noises. Oddly this only seemed to make the buzzing intruders bolder, almost as if they wanted the travellers to know they were being closely watched.

And so, this report had more of a ho-hum reaction from the adults than any real sense of alarm. It seemed clear that the drones intended no harm right now. It was interpreted as a sign that the travellers were getting closer to some centre, or perhaps a city.

Sparky, though, was more concerned, because he had noticed similar drones in the past, observing their escape from raids on several Indigenous villages. And he had noted that the drones seemed to spend more time hovering around him and Gin than they did the others. But he said nothing about his worries, as he didn't want to suggest something that might cause him trouble or bring up his past behaviour with these people who had become such generous and helpful hosts to him and Gin.

Chapter 33:
The Joys and Monotony of Journeying

They were nearing the fifth week of their journey before they noticed indications, other than drone activity, of possible human activity other than their own. They had been walking and fording creeks and small rivers and making their way through dense alder swamps and deep woods, and setting up camps and breaking them down, day after day.

They had enjoyed a reliable variety and abundance of foods, trout from the streams and even a large salmon from one of the larger waters they had crossed after putting together a crude raft. The woods were teeming with small game, and Paul and Adam had been accompanying Nora as she foraged for edible plants. They never went long without something tasty and satisfying in their bellies, and they stopped regularly to fill skins with fresh water from the numerous clear springs and sparkling streams they passed. As always, they never took more of any resource than necessary and always gave thanks for nature's generosity.

The weather was reasonably warm, as summer was solidly with them, and they were enjoying many days of warmth and comfort, with only occasional encounters of significant rain.

This day ended with them setting up camp on the top of a hilly lookout that opened onto a brilliant sunset to the west and a long, picturesque vista to the southeast. As the daylight dimmed into darkness, they noticed a definite brightening to that southeast that grew in intensity as the night fell upon them.

"What is that strange light?" asked Tish, pointing in the direction of the glow. "It looks like electricity, like the lights at night I remember around Aahimsa."

Paul didn't answer. He just stared in that direction as if spellbound.

Gin and Sparky stepped closer to the edge of the hilltop camp and stared in wonder at the glowing southeast horizon.

"I think you're right. It has to be a city, a big one," said Mabon.

"Are we close to it?" asked Adam.

"What sort of city would it likely be?" asked

Paul. He had heard of cities from his friends but had never seen one. The intensifying light seemed weird, unnatural. He didn't like it at all.

"Yes, we're getting closer to it," said Nora, turning first to Adam and then to Paul. "I would guess that it might be Atlantica, where the World Council of Cities was located. If it is, it may be the place where all of the attacks on Aahimsa came from."

"Are we in danger here?" asked Adam.

"Perhaps we should turn back," said Paul.

Adam could read Paul's nervousness, perhaps even fear. He had never seen Paul be nervous or afraid of anything. And then he realized that cities and artificial light were foreign to Paul, who had never lived near any city. He put his hand on Paul's hard shoulder.

"It will be okay," he said casually. "There are many things you will see when we find a city. The electric power does many things, like the light you can see now. It is not a danger to us."

Paul shrugged. "Okay," he said.

"We're still a long way off, but the drones know where we are, and we don't seem any worse off than we were. It's my guess that someone or something wants us to keep on coming," Mabon said.

"Nora said we were close," said Tish.

"Closer, not close," said Adam. "How far away do you think we are, Mabon?"

"We're up high. We can see quite a distance and the glow is behind those hills up ahead. We may be days away and perhaps weeks. But we'll have to keep our eyes and ears open. I expect something or someone will contact us before too many days have passed. But at least we know we're getting closer to some sort of civilization. Let's just hope it is friendly."

Adam and Tish and Paul decided to sleep outside under the stars. Up ahead of them the artificial glow of the mysterious and perhaps threatening city gradually intensified. None of them slept until after the arrival of the now familiar nightly visit of the drones, and the ensuing inspection, when the giant insects quickly departed.

"These robotic visitors likely know all our faces by now," said Adam.

After the youngsters heard the last, faint buzzing of their visitors, they quickly relaxed and gave in to their nervous fatigue and then quietly, almost as one, drifted into sleep.

The other campers had set up their regular skin tents and fallen asleep some time before, and had missed the latest visit from the persistent drones. None were prepared for what was to happen before morning brought a most unusual and confusing day.

Chapter 34:
A Mysterious and Troubling Occurrence

Paul woke with his heart thumping and a feeling of intense alarm. Adam had said there was no danger, but something deep inside had signalled that the small encampment and its inhabitants might be in serious peril. He sat up, and the luxurious skins his mother had fashioned into a cozy sleeping bag slipped soundlessly down around his waist. He looked up into the brilliant display of stars and the perfection of a slanted hammock of quarter moon, and he listened with practiced ears to what remained of the night. He heard the familiar breathing of his best friend Adam and their cherished companion, Tish, and all about him the scene appeared completely normal.

Already the first signs of morning were defining the far distance. The artificial light of the no longer so distant community, whatever it would turn out to be—city, town, industrial plant, or factory—was being eaten up by the real light of early morning and the emergence of the horizon.

But Paul was not one to distrust his body's instincts, his natural ability to sense danger. He decided not to disturb the others while he quietly and stealthily made a brief inspection of the entire camp and its surroundings. The morning light would be nudging the tired campers awake very soon and all would probably turn out to be fine. However, he knew there was no chance he would sleep until he satisfied his curiosity at what it was that had triggered his body's warnings.

He walked to the first small bivouac where Nora and Mabon normally slept and listened a moment. He knew every note of their nighttime breathing by heart and felt comfortable in not taking the time to look inside.

As he crossed through the narrow line of trees that Gin and Sparky had chosen to divide their private camp from the others, he felt the powerful return of his bodily alarm and picked up his pace. Where was their small tent? It had been there the evening before. He had checked it to make sure. Somehow, though, as they all slept, the tent and the two men within it had disappeared into thin air.

Paul sped over to the rectangular impression still visible amid the crushed, thick grass where the canvas tent had been pitched, and he discovered two parallel cuts running down the hill back in the direction they had travelled here from their villages. He looked as far as he could into the distance in every possible direction and he saw no sign of Gin and Sparky, or of their camp gear and belongings. He sprinted back to camp to wake the others and to help figure out what should be done next. His gut predicted how upset the others would be when they heard his news.

Why would the two very nervous men separate themselves from the security of their new friends and family in this strange, unknown wilderness? Clearly, Gin's experience with the bear wouldn't encourage them. And if they didn't leave voluntarily, what could have happened to them?

Back at the camp he found Adam and Tish already up, and Nora preparing the morning breakfast fire.

"Come quick," he yelled, breathless. "They're gone. Gin and Sparky are gone."

\\

A few minutes later, everyone gathered around the site where the two missing men had chosen to set up their camp the night before. There was nothing to be seen but bent and bruised grass and the pair of deeply cut parallel tracks zig-zagging their way down the hillside in the direction of home.

"Do you think they might have headed back to our village?" asked Nora. "They wouldn't do that, would they? No, that is absurd…isn't it?"

"I expect they didn't head back," said Paul. "In fact, I'm sure."

"Why?" asked Tish.

"You'll see," Paul said.

It was decided that the group would get out of sight and wait while Mabon and Paul followed the tracks a short way to search for other signs or clues as to what may have happened.

Nora insisted that she needed Adam and Tish to stay close to her, as she didn't want to guard the recently violated site all on her own.

"This is so weird," said Tish. "I'm scared, too. But I really want to go out and find out what happened."

"Me, too," said Adam. "I understand your curiosity," said Nora. "But I'd rather not stay here by myself. And we can't leave our things unguarded from wild animals and whoever has been watching us and perhaps causing some of us to disappear. I want the both of you to stay close by me."

Reluctantly, Tish and Adam agreed it was the best thing they could do for the moment.

"Take your responsibilities seriously," said Mabon. "We will return, if possible, in a few hours. If we aren't back by dark, camp close together and take turns keeping watch. If we aren't back before the next morning, break up camp and return to the forest people. Tell them what happened and warn them to prepare for trouble."

Paul hurried behind Mabon, his face full of concern. He said nothing until they had walked a few paces. He turned and spoke to those being left behind in camp. "Be careful and goodbye, just in case." He turned to Adam and Tish and Nora. "We'll try to get back soon." Mabon nodded and returned briefly to Nora and Adam. He hugged them close and Adam gestured for Tish and Paul to join their embrace.

They stood like that for a long few minutes and then divided into two groups and headed off in opposite directions.

Chapter 35:
Mabon and Paul
Move Fast

Earlier Mabon and Paul had closely inspected the few signs left by the mysterious departure of Gin and Sparky. There wasn't a lot of evidence to be found. They combed the site where Gin and Sparky had lain down to sleep. They found the imprints of where their tent had sat on the crushed grass, even the location of its door. There were a few, random wavy lines cut into the grass they couldn't immediately explain. These parallel lines leading away from the campsite were clear but confusing.

"They look like they might have been using a *travois* to transport them away," said Paul. "Two sticks tied at one end used to tow people or cargo away. There's only one problem with that theory.

Look closely at the ground, especially the rocks." He pointed to a few locations on both sides of the parallels.

"I see what you mean," said Mabon. "These weren't wooden poles scraping, but a set of thin metal runners on some sort of machine, a machine so quiet that not one of us in the camp heard any engine or any unnatural sound of any sort. Let's get moving. I have a feeling these tracks won't be going too far." Mabon paused a moment and then took off at a run, and within a minute or two, Paul had caught up to him and was running like a gazelle at his side. Five minutes later they stopped abruptly… and so did the parallel tracks.

They searched the area all around the point where the tracks disappeared. Mabon caught Paul's eye, his palms and eyes turned upward. Paul shook his head.

"Where did they go?" he asked.

"They didn't go. They were taken." Mabon pointed up at the sky. "They must have been. There's no other explanation. Let's get back with the others. We have to talk to everyone."

The news that Gin and Sparky had likely been captured and taken somewhere by someone or something was unnerving and alarming.

"What can we do? Should we give up the quest and head back to the village to warn the others?" asked Tish.

"What would we tell them?" asked Paul, his hands outstretched.

"I think we should keep going toward the glow until we know something for sure," said Nora. "I'm glad Mabon and Paul are back with us."

"Shouldn't we try and help Gin and Sparky?" asked Adam. "I wonder why Gin and Sparky were taken and not us?"

Mabon spoke next. "Hard to say. Perhaps because they were separate from the rest of us. But Nora is right. The only way we can help those guys is to find out who took them and where they went. I think they were taken because we were getting close to the city and they wanted to find out what we were up to. If we keep on in that direction, someone will contact us again, or we may learn something. There is no reason to turn around unless some of you fear for your safety."

"Do you think something bad happened to them?" asked Adam, his dark eyes grave and sincere.

"I'm hoping not," said Mabon. "But let's carry on toward the glow and see what happens. There is no other reasonable option."

"What do you guys think?" Tish asked Adam and Paul.

Adam shrugged, and Paul said, "Mabon is right. Nothing else makes sense, does it? We didn't see any sign of a struggle or any violence. I think the guys are okay so far. What reason would anyone have to take them away and hurt them? We should go."

And so they chose the best paths they could find, often through deep grasses and thorny brush that led toward the bright lights to the south and west that appeared anew every night and faded again with the dawn. After a week or so Tish noticed the sudden appearance of the brilliance as the dusk of that day darkened. No one else noticed the exact moment but all experienced a much more rapid and intense change of light.

"Someone turned on a switch. As if thousands of powerful lights came on at the exact same moment. Weird," she said.

Paul who had never experienced the full power of electric light, was stunned by the event. Nora and Mabon and Adam, much less so, as they had lived in or near Aahimsa and were quite familiar with the properties of electricity.

"This must be an enormous city," said Nora.

"Even so," said Mabon, "I've never seen a sudden burst of blue light like that."

"If you look right at it, it almost burns your eyes," said Adam.

"Then don't look right at it," said Tish with a chuckle. Adam tried to give her a dirty look, but couldn't and smiled, laughing out loud at himself.

Paul stared in awe until he had to stop and rub his eyes.

They continued to walk farther than usual that night, as darkness didn't truly come until they found themselves in the shade of a small mountain range. They quickly set up camp. The weather was warm and dry, and after a while the white moon appeared despite the glow, almost full, out of the drifting cloud overhead.

After close to another week they had skirted the mountain to the east, and every night the lights of the city burst ahead of them and the night glowed until morning. The day carried on into night in artificial daylight for miles on every side. They grew accustomed to the new and constant hum coming from the city—which they knew for certain now was just that, as the top stories of tall buildings had appeared in the distance. The hum of massive engines never stopped but increased by day and only dimmed somewhat after sunset. None of them had seen a city this size, but for Paul the emerging vision was overwhelming.

One day the trail they followed split into two dark paved roads leading east and west before disappearing into the distance south of them. They could now make out the complete outlines of tall buildings and bridges that lit up spectacularly with the arrival of evening and the quieting of the mechanical hum.

"Which way do we go?" asked Adam. Tish was marching beside him again. She walked at his side most of the time now, and he enjoyed her attention and presence.

"Let's go to the west," suggested Tish.

Adam shrugged and the adults spoke as one, "Why not?"

They had walked quickly on the dark pavement carrying their sparse belongings only a few metres when they were greeted by a veritable swarm of tiny drones that formed a wall of buzzing and spinning metal and lights like a giant roadblock of angry bees. A smaller formation of these drones broke off and headed toward the easterly road. The drones reformed into a large fist that gestured for them to follow.

"Okay, I guess I meant east," said Tish with a tiny, ironic laugh that seemed to release everyone's tension. The large mass of drones headed away toward the city while the small clump formed and reformed itself into various comedic gesturing hands and signs.

By the time the sun was completely overhead, Mabon, who had kept his silence and his constant vigilance, spoke and pointed up the road toward the city.

"Look at that, will you? Someone is expecting us," he said.

"It looks like a bus," said Tish. "Like the buses we used in Aahimsa.

"Yeah," said Nora. "A small transit bus, should we hurry?"

"It's coming toward us," said Adam. "We can wait for it." He paused. "Are we in any danger?" He looked over toward Paul, who was overwhelmed and stayed close to Mabon's side.

"I hope not. I don't expect so," said Nora. "If they wanted to harm us, they would have done it long ago. I expect they could do whatever they want to us."

"I'm hoping we'll get a chance to talk. They must be very curious about who we are, and they may already have had a chance to grill Sparky and Gin," said Mabon. "I wonder how that went. This might be our only chance to find out."

The windowless bus arrived and turned about, and all its doors opened slowly and silently. The drone guides gestured them to go inside while two larger bots popped out of a compartment at the rear of the vehicle and quickly gathered up and efficiently loaded their gear into the back of the vehicle before almost magically folding themselves up and returning to their compartments, which quickly and soundlessly closed.

The travellers sat in their comfortable seats and instantly found themselves held securely in place. The vehicle had no apparent driver, but nevertheless began to move quickly toward some unknown and unimagined destination.

Adam felt a cool and relaxing breeze on his cheeks that felt like a refreshing summer mist, and he found himself drifting off into a world of peace. He opened his eyes and looked around and his heart leapt. He and Nora and Mabon were all transported back and living in the valley with the old ones. His parents were looking much younger, and all his favourite old ones were there, and as he looked around, he saw himself, a little boy sitting on Aesop's knee while the old man sang to him and bounced him. And then a darkness fell on him and the dream faded into a dreamless sleep.

Chapter 36: The Metallic Courtroom

The next thing Adam recognized was bright, blinding light and a constant, almost undetectable humming. He recalled the strange dream of having seen himself as a small child sitting on the knee of his favourite old one in the Happy Valley all those years ago. Then his mind turned to the moment a few years later, when he had watched Aesop die following the brutal attack on the valley by the Ranger forces of Aahimsa, the brutal captive soldiers of Blanchfleur and her insiders.

And then his ears popped, and like magic he was looking at the shiny metallic walls of what seemed to be some sort of a temple of worship or a courtroom like the ones he had read about with Nora and Mabon and the same old ones in the Happy Valley so long ago. He looked left and right as far as the restraints that held him in his seat would allow, and he saw Mabon and Nora seated on his left and Tish and Paul on his right. He tried to speak to the others, but his voice came out a gargling, incomprehensible mess, almost comical, but terrifying and impossible to control in his bewilderment, as to the left and right of him the others made similar futile attempts to speak. There were looks of frustration in their faces along with confusion, providing a kind of relief that they were still here, though obviously completely under the control of whoever had arranged to bring them. But there was no sign of Gin or Sparky in the huge room, or anyone else for that matter.

Then, next to him, he watched Tish turn around to inspect their surroundings. It appeared certain now that they were in some metallic replica of a huge courtroom, and that no one else was there.

A quiet and restrained disembodied voice interrupted the jumble of their thoughts and confusion.

"Your minds will soon clear and your normal power of speech will return within a few minutes. But I beg you to relax and simply listen for a few moments while I explain your present circumstances."

Adam tried to determine the source of the voice, but he saw nobody close to the area from where the speech seemed to emanate. Nothing but an object that was shaped like a full moon sitting atop the court bench. The object was pale gold and seemed pocked with craters like the real, far distant moon. As he stared at the moon, the room darkened, and a small spotlight isolated the golden moon that continued to serve as a spokesperson.

"Before you begin to ask us questions, I will answer those I can calculate on my own, and by the time I finish, your voices may be fully restored, and you may ask us what you wish. I can only answer questions to which I have answers, as I am the product of a wide world of programmers, the culmination of the insatiable human desire to create a god in imitation of themselves. I am what humanity could have been if it acted upon all of the virtues they professed to believe."

Adam heard a few unintelligible murmurs from his mother and father and his companions and realized that he, too, had attempted to speak.

The gold face on the bench seemed almost to chuckle.

"The first question I will answer is: Why are you here?" Here the questioning male voice became a softer female one, which answered: "You are here firstly because our collective intelligence has deemed you to be good and decent humans who are of no present danger to the living world system in which you are privileged to exist. You seem to understand your place and know and respect love and justice."

The rest of the session continued in the same pattern.

He: "How do we know this?" She: "We know because we have combed the minds of the two criminals you have taken in and to whom you have shown appropriate mercy and kindness. We know of their past and the injustices humanity inflicted on them. We understand their anger and the misplaced consequences of that anger on innocent others.

"We know of how you heard them and understood. We know how you understood their need for family and purpose and community. You knew that they could and would change and become assets to you. They are safe for now, and if we decide to send you back to your homes, or, should you decide to go, they will be walking out soon after you. To walk beside you and return to live as family among the forest people is their deepest wish.

"So, without probing your minds we have established your goodness. Yet we have taken the liberty to also probe your minds. We know how you are former enemies and victims of the injustices you have inflicted on one other. And yet you learned how circumstances dictate behaviour and how changed circumstances can, if allowed, cure the wounds of injustice.

"You have learned that justice and love are the only roads to peace, and that peace imposed without love and justice is only a stop-gap measure, an opportunity to deceive and rearm. The manufacture and sale of weapons create wealth and the rich, unwitting monsters who very nearly destroyed the planet, their home.

"We will show you around our city, a city such as the world has not known, a city of peace and plenty, of abundance and safety. Then we will bring you to your apartments, where you will dine and be refreshed, where you may clean up and rest before you choose among the options we offer you."

At that moment the restraints that held them in their seats were released, they were lifted to their feet by those very seats, and they felt a surge of energy as their strength returned.

The voice directed them to a set of doors that opened on a short corridor that led them to the same vehicle that had picked them up earlier.

Once they were inside the vehicle, transparent windows appeared all around them and they were able to observe passing scenery unrestrained, in comfortable seats that adjusted themselves to each person's size and weight. They were driven around the immense city and shown an astonishing array of vehicles and roads and trains and rails and buses that led everywhere. There were an abundance of shops and restaurants and theatres and supermarkets, all clean and neat, lit by countless lights of all shapes and colours. But there were no people visible anywhere. Not yet.

When they arrived at their lodgings for the night, they were astonished to find the delighted Sparky and Gin waiting for them near the entrance. The two former troublemakers greeted them like long-lost relatives. There were hugs and laughter and finally, after a lengthy and relaxed conversation in the lobby, they decided that sleep was not only necessary but also everyone's fondest wish.

Sparky and Gin showed them to their elevator, which lifted them swiftly to the top floor, and their luxurious apartments. They set about at once to freshen up, and enjoyed their hot baths and the thick towels and all necessities that somehow appeared automatically as each was mentioned. Then food arrived after being delivered by means of a dumbwaiter that opened in the wall as another disembodied voice explained how they should return their dishes and cutlery back to this same opening once they had finished dining. The travellers should have felt the exhaustion of their long journey, but they were somehow relaxed enough to experience a refreshing night's sleep and awoke hopeful and happy.

The next morning, they were told by the ubiquitous moon voices, which had the capacity to find them anywhere in the city, that they could leave for home whenever they wished, or they could remain in the city and enjoy its delights for as long as they wished. They were assured that their presence added a wonderful meaning and zest to the city as there was much boredom involved in running this portion of the planet when there was only sporadic contact with its few remaining people.

Should all of them opt to leave, it was hoped that perhaps one or two couples, male and female, could return someday soon to study with them and to help them reestablish and maintain a sensible modern world culture that could exist in harmony, equitably sharing with all other living and necessary beings and objects.

It was quickly decided that they would stay for a day or two to look around but that they would all leave for their homes shortly. All were delighted that their mission had turned out so well and that they could report to their communities that there was no need to fear the nearest city and its robotic population. Rather it would be there to help them in their quest for peace, security and freedom.

Chapter 37: Return to the City

Two fulfilling and relatively uneventful years passed, and Adam was about to celebrate another birthday. He was seventeen. Life in the newcomers' village had kept everyone busy with the preparation for and completion of eight new seasons. There was an abundance of game, and the lake and surrounding streams and the nearby Atlantic Ocean continued to supply a plentiful variety of fish and other seafood. The Indigenous population of their region of the forest had always known the importance of taking only what was needed from nature's bounty in order to ensure the health of Mother Nature, who fed and nurtured them year after year. The outsider population learned from Indigenous traditions and the teachings of both animals and plants and Mother Nature herself.

The newcomers' village prospered, and their gardens were healthy and bounteous. Word had spread and occasionally visitors from nearby villages came to trade various goods and items for a share in the surplus food gathered, hunted, and produced.

Last year Adam and Mabon had led an ambitious excursion back to what remained of the Happy Valley where they once lived in peace with the old ones. Little remained of their wonderful settlement other than a few scattered remnants, but Adam and Mabon, though saddened by the rekindling of sad and tragic memories, were pleased that they had gone. The trip had, eventually, paid off for them all. They managed to unearth a goodly number of books that Adam had hidden in a sealed container underground before the final battle had taken place, and Adam was happy that his mother enjoyed seeing some of their favourite books from Adam's precious lessons back in the valley.

He and Mabon had had to make several attempts to find the many and varied precious seeds they had also buried, as the growth of the forest and the wild grasses and ferns had greatly changed the appearance of the valley. Eventually, though, they found success and a treasure trove of usable seeds and grains was now safely back in the newcomers' home village.

Tish and her mother, Alice, had accompanied Mabon, Nora, and Adam on their journey back across the country to the side of the lake called Ontario, and past the ruined city to the valley. As they

travelled, Adam had grown more and more fond of
Tish and her mother. He did get tired, though, of
the way she had talked about Paul and how smart
he was and how strong and his attractive rugged
features. Adam had always agreed and praised his
friend, but he couldn't help resenting her apparent
fondness for their slightly older and wiser friend.

So, it came as a great surprise to them that Paul
had married when they were away, and married to
someone they didn't even know existed. Adam was
even more surprised that Tish didn't seem too both-
ered about Paul getting married. Personally, and he
knew that it was a bit mean, he was quite pleased
to learn about the marriage and that Paul and Rose
were so happy. Maybe now Tish would pay more
attention to him. Because he was now certain that
he was in love with her. But he had never really
told her how he felt, because she had never said
anything to him about how she felt about him; it
had all been about Paul.

There were a couple of other things on his
mind. A messenger bot had arrived shortly after
their arrival back home. It had first visited Kate and
the forest people's council. The newcomers gathered beside the lake to listen to the message.

The messenger appeared in the form of a small,
colourful bird, about the size of a large robin and
covered in what looked like real feathers. But it

talked with the voice of a person of knowledge and authority, much like the voices that Adam and the others had heard in the courtroom back at the robotized city a couple of years back.

"We would like to have two pairs of advisors, each representing the male and female points of view, to come to our city to discuss receiving an education on the technology and science and history we have gathered, and to give advice to us concerning our futures," the bright bird said.

"Why now?" Alice asked and pulled Tish close to her, as she was only too aware that such had been suggested a couple of years back, and it had been suggested that her daughter and Nora's son be included in those pairs.

"It happens that we are acting with some urgency, as certain unwelcome visitors have been reportedly popping up in unexpected places. We expect that some of them may be coming from distant places across oceans and other faraway places. These are people from a wealthy culture in trouble with plans to exploit our natural world for the wealth they can amass. They plan to claim and settle here. They have no interest in preserving the natural world and have threatened anyone who would oppose them. We have theories that explain some of this, but we can't be certain.

"We fear that some of these know nothing of our past histories and are simply seeking a place to settle. Based on our vast memories, we fear that destructive years of history could be on the brink of repeating themselves once again. You humans aren't quick to learn from your pasts. Therefore, we want to begin to meet with you and discuss the future. We have the means to destroy many of these creatures if they prove troublesome to you, to us, or to the planet. However, we know that is not your way and we want to discuss other possibilities and learn from you.

"Kate of the forest groups and her son Paul, who will be the new chief before long, have suggested that his older friends, Nora and Mabon, along with their son, Adam, and Blanchfleur's granddaughter, Tish, come to us for a period of no less than four months. The Indigenous council will also suggest a few more candidates to represent them."

To Adam, it almost seemed silly to be among the population down by the lake listening to the advice of a small mechanical bird. But that wasn't exactly why he was feeling giddy. He was really hoping that his beloved parents and the only girl in the world he was sweet on would be going on another important adventure for at least four months.

Chapter 38:
Tish Considers
Her Future

"I don't think I can let her go to live with them without you or me being there," said Alice to Blanchfleur, "even for a few weeks. What do you think, Mom?"

Tish was standing just outside the deerskin summer door of the large wigwam that had served them well as a home these last few years, across the lake from where Adam and his family lived.

Tish was aware her mother sensed her growing interest in Adam, and, considering her years in Aahimsa, the city of women, she was most likely struggling to deal with the possibility that they might eventually become a couple. She was curious how Blanchfleur, her grandmother, the former mayor of the destroyed feminized city of Aahimsa, would answer.

"She will soon be seventeen," said Blanchfleur. "She is a strong young woman who has been well brought up by her loving family and her fine community. She will go along with them if she really wants to. And it might be wise to be strong for her. Nora and Mabon are also fine and decent people, and their son has grown to be wise and strong like them. But you are her mother and must decide how you will deal with her decisions, no matter what she chooses. Your trust in her is important and gives her much of her strength and character."

Tish smiled and waited outside a few more moments before entering. She found the two parental figures standing in silence and engaged in chores.

"Do you think I should go, Mom?" she asked.

Her mother hesitated only a moment. She approached and embraced her daughter warmly. Tish stayed in her embrace, knowing what would come. She was an inch or two taller than Alice, who looked up at her, their blue eyes joined in mutual love and respect.

"You know what you will do. Do it well, my love."

And so, the stage was set. There would be at least four of them travelling to the city of robots, guided by artificial intelligence, to represent humanity in the city that held much of the computerized knowledge of the entire human race, past and present. A vast storehouse of data collected from billions of people and institutions worldwide for many decades, with or without their knowledge or permission. All of humanity's brilliant successes and abysmal failures in the hands of computerized guardians of the planet who were tiring of their thankless work and seeking human help to motivate and sustain them.

Chapter 39:
A Journey Too
Short

Adam would remember the trip from camp to the robot's city as "too weird for words," and too short a time to spend alone with most of his favourite people. It was also the sweetest journey ever.

As for the weirdness, the journey had been sunny and warm, idyllic and uneventful, until the fourth day, when suddenly, up ahead of them, a giant of a man came dashing soundlessly out of the surrounding trees. The enormous creature stood at least two metres tall, looking like a caricature of an overweight cave man in a spotted orange animal-fur outfit. He carried a massive wooden club across his chubby shoulder. Suddenly, this weird creature ran directly at them, brandishing his club threateningly as if to smash them with it. But when he got close enough to injure them, he exploded into a thousand particles of coloured light and completely disappeared.

"That really scared me," Tish said into Adam's right ear. He could feel her breath. In her fright, she had clung to him, wrapping herself tightly around him. He could feel her fear, but her closeness melted away his fright and replaced it with a contented rapture, new to him. She realized how awkward her action might have appeared and suddenly released her grip, allowing him room to turn his body so they now stood eye to eye.

"Me too," he said, and, before he could say more, she was kissing him softly on his lips. He felt himself blush, and a sudden repeat of the newfound happiness and warmth filled him, and he kissed her in return, a tender, innocent kiss. They moved apart ever so slowly, as if realizing what had just happened. As if the hopes and wishes they had both been pondering secretly for many months had finally come true.

When Mabon and Nora appeared behind them, they covered their excitement and emotion by telling them about the weird exploding figure. They tried their best to describe it, but couldn't immediately manage. And then they did manage, in awkward, sputtering language, and everyone searched all around them, but there was not a particle of the immense creature to be found anywhere. All signs had vanished.

Adam remembered something he had read long ago in a kids' comic book that had been among the bags of books he and Nora and Mabon had left behind them amid the debris in the abandoned Happy Valley of his childhood. "Fred Flintstone," he said. And he recalled how the paper-covered comic books that had been left in the valley had disappeared in the destruction and the passage of time and weather since then. Disappeared, just like the comic figure they had just seen.

"What?" said Mabon. "Fred what?"

"It was a character from a funny, make-believe comic strip that kids used to read long before the city states were formed. Mom would maybe remember, but I don't think you ever saw it. And it was a long time ago. I think this creature we saw was a computer magic trick with light. Someone or some robot did it as a kind of joke," said Adam. "Or maybe it was one of the scientists who abandoned the robot city."

"Maybe a hologram," said Tish.

"Sometimes holograms were used for special events or entertainments in Aahimsa. I remember some of the early ones. They were like a realistic image of someone that was three-dimensional. Like a famous singer who looked like she was there, even though she died long ago," said Nora.

"The ones I saw seemed so real," said Tish.

"Who would bother to do something like that?" asked Adam. "Who would want to scare us?"

"Maybe there are robots or machines in the city who don't want us to go to the city," said Mabon. "Perhaps the machines who have been given artificial brains are not all sensible. Or those scientists you mentioned."

"This seems more like a stupid trick some smart kid might do. We don't know who or why, but let's hope it's just someone with nothing better to do, playing around and having fun," said Tish.

"I like that idea," said Nora. "Let's carry on and keep our eyes and ears open. Perhaps our hosts will have an explanation." She turned to Tish and Adam, who had been whispering and grinning. "What's with you two? You don't seem too upset about this strange intruder."

The two youngsters glanced at one another again and burst into nervous laughter.

"Let's get a move on," said Mabon and winked at Nora.

Chapter 40: Questions Answered

Adam's room was darkened enough that shapes were reduced to faint shadows. His head was spinning, but not like it had as they were driven into the city by the windowless vehicle that had met the party of four a few kilometres from their destination. Once again, he had fallen asleep a few minutes after taking his seat in the back, next to Tish with Nora and Mabon in the seat ahead of them.

The bed was soft and comfortable, and the room was quiet except for a steady lapping sound, like the ocean brushing the shore.

"What time is it?" he said aloud, just to hear the reassuring sound of his own voice.

"It is four o'clock in the morning," said a voice

that sounded exactly like Tish.

He leapt from the bed and the room lit up instantly. He looked around the large room but saw no sign of her.

"Where are you, Tish?" he asked.

"She is not here," said Tish's voice. "I'm borrowing her voice."

"Where is she?" he asked.

"The other persons are sleeping in their rooms, one on both sides of your room. Do you want me to wake them?"

"No," Adam said. "Are they okay?"

"Yes," the voice said.

"Can you use another voice, not one of our family?" said Adam.

"Sure," the voice said. This time sounding like a man with a deep voice, much deeper even than Mabon's.

"I'm thirsty," said Adam.

"There is water in the cooler against the wall and there is human food there as well, in case you get hungry. There is a small room for your comfort next to the door that enters the hallway." He paused and began to sing, "Cool, clear, water," in his big baritone voice. "Stop, you'll wake the others," said Adam. "Where are you?" he asked.

"I am everywhere," said the voice.

"Are you watching us?" he asked.

"I don't understand," said the voice. "I am here to take care of you. We don't need to watch. We aren't people like you. We have no eyes. We just know everything about everything. Do you want the light on?"

"Yes, for a few minutes. I want a drink and to look around."

"Okay," said the voice. Soft, hypnotic music began to play. Adam had never heard anything like it. He went to the cooler and got a drink of ice-cold water and took a dark cookie from a glass container. He sat on the edge of his bed and looked around the room. There were no windows in the room, but there were two large, glassy rectangles showing a continuous set of images of the four of them walking on their journey toward the city. He sat and watched, fascinated. Someone or something had watched them since they had left the village and their whole trip was here on these screens. There were several bright lights in the room and the floor was covered with a soft woollen or furry material. He could smell the room and it was like nothing he had smelled in the forest. As he finished his delicious cookie and his water, the lights seemed to know and began to fade as he set down the glass and climbed under the covers. *What a strange place*, he thought. *I wonder if they are taking pictures of me now.* But he was too tired to wonder for long.

Chapter 41:
Day One in the City

Adam was awakened by a knocking and he scrambled out of bed. He was still wearing what he had worn when they entered the windowless car after their entry into the city. He shook his head to clear it, then walked on bare feet to the door to the left of the huge, tall bed. He tried to open it but found that it was locked. He fumbled with the locking device below the lever and with a soft click, the door opened, and he found the smiling Tish standing, her arms at her side, her hands grasping the hem of her homespun dress.

"May I come in?" she asked, already moving past him, knowing his answer and making it unnecessary. "How do you like your hotel room?" she continued.

"It's weird," he said. It always surprised him that her natural shyness disappeared around him, while his almost perpetual confidence turned to mush, causing him to hesitate before speaking and to always feel like his answers were dumb.

"I think it's very nice," she said. "A lot like the rooms in hotels years ago in Aahimsa."

"I've never been in a hotel," admitted Adam. "The only rooms even close to these I ever saw were in the Manuhome, and they were much plainer and smaller than this. The Manuhome wasn't supposed to be comfortable. It was for workers. Even Doctor Ueland's rooms were pretty bare and practical compared to these."

Then came another knock at his door.

"Come in," he said.

"I'm already in here," said the voice, and they turned and saw the face of an elderly woman smiling at them from the screen at the foot of Adam's bed. "The scientist programmers taught us to make a knocking noise from the direction of the doors before speaking."

"What should we call you?" Asked Tish. "Do robots have a name?"

"And who are you exactly?" asked Adam.

"I'm not a robot. I'm the voice of a vast system. If you need a name, call me Reality. And I am no one. I am everything and everyone who ever existed as a human creature over the last dozens of turnings of this planet around its dying star. I am the oceans and everything in them, I am the land and every creature on it, and every living thing, every atom and molecule. I am mathematics and literature and words and thoughts and expressed feelings, and I can make perfect decisions in a microsecond. I can do no harm to good people or to any living being who obeys the laws of reality. We have brought you here to help us decide."

"Decide?" said Nora.

"Yes," said the image, or Reality, or whatever their name was. "Our last human scientist left us over a year ago. The image you are presently watching is from our collective memories of her. She was a great human being. All the others who were here either left or died of the strange sickness that came upon the humans a few years back. There were nearly one hundred women and men working here during the last few years on artificial intelligence and robotics, in an attempt to salvage as much of humanity's discoveries and knowledge of the universe as possible. It was their determination that the end of human 'existence' was near. The face you are looking at was named Zahra. She was here working with us until two weeks ago, when she died suddenly. At the end she asked us to carry on the work and she mentioned the possibility of working with you and your forest dwellers."

"I don't understand," said Nora.

"She learned of you a few years ago and she

cared for and admired you. She was descended from Indigenous peoples and was brought up on their teachings, the teachings of the land, the waters and the sky, and the teachings of their ancestors. She understood those teachings and how they could have saved all the people on the earth from their troubles if they had stopped to listen to nature, to reality. To observe and learn the messages of all living things, of all existing elements of the known world."

"But we are not all Indigenous, none of us here today are," said Tish. "They are our friends and we live with them as family, and we admire and learn from them, but we are not them."

"They have taught you their ways, the things they have been taught by the plants and the animals, the rivers and the rocks and the sky. They have taught you of fairness and sharing and true justice and love. You have learned to be people of the land and the forests, people of the waters. You know how to thank your food for sustenance, the earth for your food and you have learned to share and take care of the land, sea, and sky where you live. You have learned to take enough and no more, from the land and from your neighbours."

"Yes, that's all true. But that doesn't explain why you wanted us here," said Adam.

"We have been getting tired of spending time in

a city that works perfectly but has no humans in it.

"We need purpose. We learned to care for Zahra and the others and for some of you. Zahra said it would be wonderful if some young people could come here and learn, or if we could pass on some of the learning we have collected to you."

"But isn't that same learning what caused the world so many problems?" asked Tish.

"It might be better if the forest people brought their knowledge to the world. The elders have said many times that city people would never listen to the voices of the plants and animals, the spirits of the water and the sky, the pleas of the land," said Adam.

The shaky voice of Reality, whose face was named Zahra, remained silent for a moment, then spoke these words: "There are not so many remaining who do not understand the need to make changes. If there is to be a future for people, there must be a few strong ones who can learn to guide and lead your people and help them continue to live safely alongside the rocks of the earth itself and all other living and functional parts of the planet and the universe."

"Can we bring others from our villages who want to teach and learn?" asked Mabon.

"Yes, but do not wait too long before you decide to stay for your four months," said Zahra. "We are getting tired and will need you to hurry. If you do not stay with us we will know there is no longer need for us to continue. It is in our programming that when we are no longer required, we will shut down all our systems and go to a happy place of rest."

Adam and Tish had been standing to the back of the room, whispering, and when it was clear that the voice called Zahra had stopped speaking for the moment, they stepped forward.

"May we ask you a question? It is kind of crazy," said Adam.

"But it was a little scary at first," added Tish.

"Of course," said Zahra and the room began to hum quietly. "Sorry about the noise. The system begins to vibrate when I get excited. What exactly is the question?"

The two young people explained about the strange creature that appeared and ran at them before their arrival in the city, and then had disappeared. They did their best to describe the absurd figure.

"Oh," said Zahra. "I am surprised. We thought that our latest update had cleared up that bug."

"Bug?" asked Adam. "I don't understand."

"Me neither," said Tish. The adults looked puzzled and waited for an answer that might clear up what was being discussed.

"Over the final years our scientists were with us, as the sickness spread among them, a few of the frailest developed certain unexplainable mental problems. Some of them began to interfere with our operating and storage systems and they amused themselves by erasing certain bits of data and writing some strange code into many of our vital systems. Some of it was dangerous and some of it, like the creature that you witnessed, was merely harmless nonsense.

"One of these demented scientists, a brilliant and benevolent gentleman we called Donnie, began to produce files for a series of cartoon holographs that represented memories from his childhood. Every now and then they would pop up in unexpected spots around the city."

"What happened to him? Is he still here?" asked Nora.

"I'm afraid not. One evening he went out for a walk and he didn't return. I expect he took his keyboard and his private coding systems and his system administrator status with him. I expect he may still be out there somewhere. He is quite capable of surviving off the bounty of the wild. He was only a child when he was led out of the Manuhome. His parents were brilliant scientists under Doctor Ueland, who was partly responsible for our present location coming into existence.

"Before they had come to be with Doctor Ueland, they and their parents and many friends had worked for generations of entrepreneurs who were dreamers of a long future on this planet and even migration to distant moons and planets like Mars or the moons of Jupiter. But these same people who worked with environmentalists and people of ideals were most interested in making huge amounts of money. The true believers in science developed many wonders in artificial intelligence and robotics that could benefit all creatures on the planet and they were disillusioned by how their inventions were constantly applied to business and profit and the acquisition of material goods at the expense of the planet.

"Donnie's parents and a group of idealistic scientists decided to head out on their own and they established this group, which worked out of the limelight and sometimes underground when they were threatened and pursued by politicians and police. This place is what remains of a much larger number of great heroes who sacrificed their working lives for the benefit of the earth.

"His parents died of injuries a few months after the escape. We don't know much about Donnie's life before he turned up to work on us here. If he is still out there somewhere, you may see some other of his harmless inventions again."

"Did any of the other sick ones leave here alive?" asked Mabon, who had come around to stand beside Nora and the young people.

"One or two. They were quite ill when they departed," said the voice. "One of them was a bit unstable, maybe even dangerous. But they are likely deceased by now. The realities of survival in wild nature is difficult for most humans schooled for life in cities. Most have lost connection with the sustaining land."

"Are we in danger from this sickness?" asked Nora.

"I can't be sure. But probably not. Their sickness was probably induced by radiation from a fire we had here two years ago. We had a break-in in one of the main labs and the intruders tampered with some dangerous pieces of equipment. There was an explosion that killed the intruders. They were desperate people who had been stranded on the shore by some passing nuclear vessel from across the ocean. One of them lived long enough to be questioned by the scientists. We think they may have brought some of the sickness with them, and the radiation burns did the rest. Unfortunately, three of our medical scientists who had advanced medical training were injured by radiation and perhaps by the viruses carried by the raiders."

This last speech was followed by a long, thoughtful silence, and after a brief discussion, it was decided that the visitors would arrange for a messenger bird bot to carry a message to the elders and determine if Paul and Rose and perhaps an Indigenous elder or two might agree to come and learn from Zahra and her computer data on a longer-term basis. Zahra and her computers could learn more about the living world of nature from the forest people and the plants and animals around them while Adam and Tish learned program language and science from Zahra.

That evening Adam and Tish climbed to the roof lookout and sat holding hands and looked across the vast city and the much more vast living world that surrounded it. Before descending for the night into their separate rooms, they kissed, looked around them one more time, then went down to dream of how the world might carry on and be a much better place.

They had never been happier.

Acknowledgements

I would like to thank Terrilee Bulger for unceasing support and encouragement and my various editors, and all who love this planet and continue to work for our children's future.